Surf

Also by Kyle Bern

. . . and the kids: A Disorientation Guide for the College-Bound

Surf

Kyle Bern

authorHOUSE®

AuthorHouse™
1663 Liberty Drive
Bloomington, IN 47403
www.authorhouse.com
Phone: 1-800-839-8640

Published by AuthorHouse   06/18/2013

ISBN: 978-1-4817-6667-8 (sc)
ISBN: 978-1-4817-6668-5 (e)

Library of Congress Control Number: 2013911114

Any people depicted in stock imagery provided by Thinkstock are models, and such images are being used for illustrative purposes only.
Certain stock imagery © Thinkstock.

This book is printed on acid-free paper.

Because of the dynamic nature of the Internet, any web addresses or links contained in this book may have changed since publication and may no longer be valid. The views expressed in this work are solely those of the author and do not necessarily reflect the views of the publisher, and the publisher hereby disclaims any responsibility for them.

For my mom

Surf

He adored surfing, as he did almost everything else about the beach. The gleaming white gulls which he would chase in the sand. The cats slinging hotdogs to hungry cats on the strip. The cats with metal detectors, hoping for that one big score beneath the sands. The cats driving motorized carts, some of them old or fat, some just lazy, the sand grazing their furs. His surfing brethren, which he loved like his own family, each of them mounting boards and throwing themselves into aqua voids, skimming over and hopping through and lunging within the water.

He romanticized the beach with every fur on his body. The beach was his home, mother, teacher, offering up all the kindness, care, and instruction he could have ever asked for. When the days turned to night he and his surfing brethren would ascend from the beach to the boardwalks above it, and spend their nights in shacks which served as their homes. Then they'd get up, wake up, and do it all over again. He wouldn't have it any other way. The cats on roller blades making zippy, multicolored streaks down the boardwalk. The cats on skateboards, navigating the different types of pavement and railing that constituted the infrastructure of the beach. The cats on dirtbikes, bunnyhopping the curbside. All underneath a clear blue sky that seemed to stretch forever. The beach was his beach, there was no place he'd rather be. Little the cat: king of the beach!

One afternoon Little was awakened by the telephone. The voice on the other end announced itself as Sirse, Little's friend and mentor.

"Hola, como estas!" Little howled into the receiver.

"Hello, Little. I'm doing fine. Just fine," came the reply.

Little yawned, licked a furry leg. "So, what can I do for you?"

"It's a little business down by the club tonight. Not really a big deal. Just some business."

Little nodded to himself, and then he responded: "far out".

"So you think you can do it?"

"I don't see why not."

This time it was Sirse who responded: "far out".

Two hours later when Sirse called him back, Little was drinking an iced milk and was getting ready to hear a proposal. At the time he didn't know he was getting ready to hear a proposal; he only knew he was drinking iced milk. But when Sirse whispered at him, "I have a proposal for you, kitty cat," all became evident.

"How much and what's the place," Little asked, trying to remain casual, lowering his tumbler of milk from his chin.

"It's that place north across the park, by the construction site. It'll only take an hour or two," Sirse's jazzy whisper of a voice danced its way toward him.

"I'll be there." Little slammed the receiver down into an old-fashioned rotary dial phone. A loud ringing rang through the apartment. Little kicked back in his creaky wooden chair and contemplated the situation.

Sirse's proposal faced Little with a potentially sticky situation. It wasn't that Little didn't trust, his friend, exactly; it was more that trouble (and rotten rumors) seemed to follow Sirse like kitties following the Pied Piper. Racketeering, embezzlement, fraud—the cat had a police record as long as his arm. And yet for all the time Little knew Sirse, Sirse had been the most earnest, dependable, *honest* friend Little could ask for. Who but Sirse bailed Little out of jail when he got too wild on Mardi Gras? Who paid his insurance, heating, *and* electricity bills when he couldn't do it himself? More importantly, who provided Little with a place to sleep and guidance as a surfing instructor when Little first moved to the beach? It was Sirse, every time.

Little twirled his chair around, brought the iced milk to his lips, withdrew it. So then why did he still not trust Sirse, not fully? There where those rotten rumors, constantly tailing Sirse like the cat's pitch black shadow. It wasn't just the embezzlement charges. It was the rumors of something worse, something Little didn't care to think about, that prevented him from falling asleep, in that apartment with the sun setting through the windows, as he waited for the job that late evening.

[*Foreigner, or: Little's Dream # 1*

Disarming young toms come to female callers as per tradition, and suddenly everything is sparkling and glimmering in the night air above. Cats in tuxedos tap dance across keyboards, chasing bouncy balls and balls of yarn. Meanwhile a searing red sun burns; it's a powerful sun, a sun that burns earth. Cats scream and meow in the distance, desperate for salvation. But there is none. The fire only rises.]

Little is already shaking his head with his paw when he realizes he woke with the nightmare still in his head. He thinks of the fire, remembers the screams from his cat, and is up and pacing his apartment within seconds.

He licks his lips, his paws, rubs his paws over his eyes, and struggles to think. But thinking isn't easy when you're a cat, not this kind of thinking. What caused this awful nightmare and what does it mean? Little strains to remember to back before he fell asleep and lands on Sirse.

Sirse's moral ambiguity announced itself through every aspect of the feline's physique, from his slippery, side-to-side gait to his jet black coat. The animal walked as if his back legs were damaged, often sliding the lower half of his body across the floor as he walked. But Little wasn't the shallow type, wasn't known to judge a cat based on superficial qualities. What, then, made the creature so nervous?

It probably was just a Barter of the rumors that Little would like to consider himself better than but couldn't put behind himself. Sirse wasn't exactly the most well-liked cat on the beach; then again, he also wasn't *not* the most well-liked, plus he was *definitely* the most connected. Things other cats had to pay for on the beach, Sirse and his crew got for free—surfboards, swimming trunks, helmets, all kinds of sports gear. So there was really nothing to worry about, was there? Little laced up his boots and prepared for the job.

Licking his fur down into a smooth sheen, Little tucked his leg fur under his cargo pants, and his cargo pants under his boots. Leaning over the bed he checked his chucks, standard issue for this assignment. He admired the handiwork which he himself had done earlier that week: a tattoo on his belly of a tomcat with legs spread, jerking off his own boner. The penis was erect, its molecules stabbing at the air around them. The image was a symbol of Little's belief in individuality and personal freedom. Satisfied, Little grunted, then flipped over into a standing position. Easy, relax, no problem. He could do this assignment in his sleep, he figured. So he got in the Toyota and started the engine.

Across town, Little got out of his car and began to stalk an alley that ran along the side of the building. He climbed some scaffolding then got to the roof. Running to the other side of the roof, Little looked down to see Sirse's Lexus parked on the street. So Sirse was here. That meant it was time for Little to get into place.

The cat ran back to the scaffolding and began to tear off the advertising signs that had been plastered to the wall. Little would stretch these signs across the metal poles of the scaffolding, blocking off the sightlines for whatever

Sirse wanted to do in this alley. Soon, more cats arrived to help Little. He didn't recognize them and they didn't introduce themselves. Little could only scratch his belly and wonder: what the hell *were* they doing here? Sirse had never brought in the cats on assignments this involved. If anything Sirse had always wanted them to have as much of a hands-off approach as possible. What the hell was Sirse doing?

Just then there was gunfire below. Little looked over the edge to see Sirse's driver backing into the car, then the car leaving the alley and screeching off into the distance. Little felt sick. He felt dizzy. He lay down on his back on the scaffolding. The other cats scremed and panicked, now on their way down rafters and wooden planks. Little began to ease himself onto a pole near him; gently, gently. He slowly, tenderly made his way down the scaffolding. Finally he made it to the street. He struggled into the Toyota, grabbing his head. When he finally got in he lay back and just breathed deep, occasionally wheezing. He finally turned on the engine on his car and swerved home.

Back at his apartment, Little took a pill for his head and then passed out in the dark.

Little awoke. His headache of the previous night had turned into a full-fledged migraine and he lay in the bed, screaming, spitting, hissing in agony. He fumbled around the nightstand, knocked over a clock, and, finally, reached his paw onto a bottle of aspirin. Little rocked back on his feet, preparing to make the necessary journey across the room. He tucked the bottle deeper into his paw and made a dash from the bedroom to the bathroom, throwing open the bathroom door with his face. Little squinted in the dim light of the bathroom; he saw weird light patterns and geometric shapes and floaty things moving in front of his eyes. He squinted harder and, sweating, got the faucet on. He shook out three pills and shoved them into his mouth, then took a deep, long drink from the faucet. Little backed into a wall and slid down to the floor, panting. He grabbed his head with two fists and shook it. Slowly, he stood up and walked back into the bedroom. He gathered his "hang loose" t-shirt and a pair of Bermuda shorts and pulled them on over his white fur with black spots. He had to try not to think right now, had to clear his mind and just get to the beach. He just had to get to the beach to talk to Sirse and figure out what happened. That's all he had to do. So he walked outside and emptied his thoughts and got in his car.

On the way to the beach Little tuned into some sort of conspiracy theorist radio. People were talking about environmental tragedies and national tragedies and international tragedies and how the United States Federal Government, specifically the President of the United States himself, was responsible for all of that. Little turned off the radio and kept driving. He was in a cold sweat. He didn't know why these programs would rattle him so, but they did. He thought it had something to do with: *They just can't be true, can they? They just can't be true.*

Little parked the Toyota on the boardwalk and got out. He walked into a nearby surf shop and grabbed a new helmet. He tried it on, decided it was awesome-snazzy enough, and left without paying. This was how commerce worked at the beach: there were shops, and there was buying and selling, but there was no strictly enforced monetary system. Paying was more a suggestion than anything. Little realized, half way to the car, that he forgot his board. This was a problem. He could pay for a replacement helmet, but no way could he afford a new board. So he got in the car and drove all the way back home. When he got there, there was a mysterious sighting inside the first floor sitting toom. There was a man, a man with bulging back eyes and a face pained white, inside the first floor of Little's house, then he disappeared. Little froze. He thought of his options: Call Sirse. Trouble was, that required going into the house for the phone. Go look for Sirse at the beach. This seemed like the best idea, since going into the house know was unthinkable. So Little got in the Toyota and drove.

He drove with the windows rolled down and tears streaming against his face. He drove like a cat with nothing left to lose, but that's only because he tended to become overly alarmed at unexplainable situations. By the time he reached the main stretch of road passing by the beach, Little was running his paw through sweaty fur, brushing the fur back away from his eyes. He scanned the strip for a parking spot and found one right by one of the beach's entrances. Little pulled over, swerving between lanes, and jammed his car into a parallel park. Little got out of the car, panting so hard he choked. He slammed the door. He headed for the beach.

The beach was a brightly lit carnival of psychedelia. Cats launched themselves off trampolines into neon star sign. Cats rode flashing jet skis; spiraling through the air they'd explode into a glittery neon haze. Cats panted over a high-speed game of Frisbee, their eyes a bacchanal of primary colors and videotechnology. And of course, cats launched themselves into insane, psychedelic water vorticies, becoming molded to the contours of their boards and the waves they road.

Little watched the surfers and licked his lips. He was tempted to grab a board and head into the fray. But not today. Today he had business to take care of.

Little walked the length of the boardwalk, ducking into shops to check for Sirse, keeping his eyes out for Sirse along the main drag. When his search turned up nothing he walked down to the beach and walked along the water in the other direction. Little was getting restless when he spotted movement in the muck at the end of the beach strip. This was the filthiest, slimiest part of the beach, the part no cat their right right mind would set foot in. Yet there were cats in there now. And as Little walked closer he recognized one of them: There was Sirse, splashing around in goop almost too thick to splash around in, goop like crude oil, sticking to and hanging off his fur in nauseating clumps. Little got closer.

"What the hell are you doing in there Sirse? This part of the beach is poison!"

"Poison only to those who haven't taken my brand new serum yet, Little my boy! Poison only to the cats who didn't get the serum!"

"And who got the serum, exactly?"

Little felt dizzy again, with a headache that was giving him chills.

9

"Anyone who pays for it of course!" Sirse cackled.

Little froze. Sure Sirse acted as a benefactor for his friends, and sure, a type of monetary system did exist on the beach, but it wasn't mandatory. Nobody paid who didn't want to, and nobody who didn't pay got less.

Sirse cackled again. "I'm just fucking with you, Little," he said briskly. "I've set up a new stand on the boardwalk that's giving out free immunizations now. It's all clean. Well, besides the fact that I stole it from that plant we infiltrated yesterday!"

Sirse wheezed laughing so hard it sounded like he might puke. Little was so relieved that he hardly had time to notice the creature flitting through the water next to Sirse. The animal raised its head, but its head was covered in goop. It approached shore, stood on two legs, made itself definitely recognizable as a cat, and extended a mucky paw in Little direction. The smaller cat's mysterious, gloopy body oozed gloop. Little got some on his paw and awkwardly tried to wash it off in the water without appearing impolite. What emerged, finally, dripping gunk though it was, was a luscious, full-bodied, able young tom. Sirse froze as the hallucinatory image came closer: the tom with chiseled abs, perfect lats and pecs, well-tousled shoulder-length blonde hair. The tom stood there amidst the surf watching Little. Little tried not to watch both. Suddenly, Sirse came over, interrupting all cats.

"Little," Sirse said. "This is Larcey."

"But you can call me Larce," Larcey said, extending a paw, grinning.

Little admired the cat. Young, tender, yet well-muscled limbs, joined a to-die-for bod in the meeting of the millennium: Little practically needed a bib he was drooling so hard. Gently, Little fingered his stiff erection beneath his swimming trunks. *Oh yes,* Little purred to himself, *he will do nicely.*

"Little," barked Sirse. "Why don't you take a walk with your new . . . er . . . companion here. Meanwhile, I have to check up on the immunization devices I set up."

Sirse hobbled down the beach, the bottom half of his legs twisting and sliding in all directions. Little looked at the evening sun gracing the face of his new surfing brother . . . and perhaps so much more.

Little and Larcey began walking along the beach and Little hit him with a barrage of questions: When did Larcey first arrive at the beach, did he like it here, how did he meet Sirse, was he involved in many of Sirse's operations; all met with a barrage of answers: Two weeks ago, loved it, on the strip when he first arrived, a few, but not many. Little would have dug into this last line of questioning had he not been so taken by the young Tom and his body. As Little and Larce walked along the beach, Little risked putting an arm around Larce's waist. Larcey squealed twice and nuzzled into Little. Little smiled and his entire face became warm.

"I should buy you a beer, kid," Little said, his voice so mellow it was like melting marshmallow.

"I don't drink . . . um . . . sir," Larcey said, hesitant.

Little grinned even wider. He didn't drink either. How perfect.

With one arm around the younger cat's shoulder, Little slowly guided Larcey along the beach until they reached a cliff-face with a reasonable-sized inlet in it. Little and Larcey stood around the opening, brushing away strands of seaweed with loose sticks in the area. Then the cats moved deeper into the opening. From inside the inlet they were able to get rid of more brush and debris. Sun shined into the cavern, forming a half circle that illuminated their presence there.

Then Little threw his stick aside, grabbed Larcey's shoulders, and began to pull him down into the sand.

Little stuck one big finger in between Larcey's teeth. Larcey bit down gently, and then harder. Larcey began sucking on Little's finger, sucking and pulling with his teeth. Larcey was, at this point, lying on his side, greedily accepting Little's finger into his mouth. Then, slowly, Little placed his opposite hand on the top of Larcey's torso and eased the cat flat down into the sand, onto the cat's back. Little then mounted Larcey across the waist and, with the hand opposite the one being sucked on, began to massage the cat's pecs and abs, working his hand in a circle. Little brought a bottle of baby oil out of the back pocket of his swimming trunks and used the oil to lube up Larcey's chest and abs. Then he held Larcey's face at a distance and watched Larcey suck on his big finger like the most innocent baby in the world . . . and then Little slammed Larcey's face into his groin.

Larcey's face felt Little's boner through mesh swimming trunks. Little rubbed Larce's face against the airhole in the trunks where cock didn't make contact with trunks but the trunks were tented, then he forced Larce's mouth around the bulge itself in the trunks. The ribbed interior of Larcey's mouth made swishy contact with the swimming trunks. Then Little pulled aside the trunks with one finger and allowed knotted black pubic hair to untangle itself into the world. His cock was undeniably hard and throbbing. Larcey bit at the swimming trunks, trying to remove them with his teeth. It was then that Larcey spotted the tattoo on Little's stomach of a man jerking off his erection.

"Whoa," Larcey said. "That is by far the raddest tattoo I have ever seen in my life."

Little grinned. "I'm glad you like, dude," he whispered.

Little paused to allow Larcey to run his fingers over the tattoo on his abs and Larcey took greedy, hungry strokes of Little's flesh. Finally, Little softly pushed away Larcey's fingers and grabbed the back of Larcey's head, easing Larcey's head into the gap he was creating in his swimming trunks. Larcey began to suck the cum out of Little's cock. Little bounced up and down on his hind legs, sending his cock flying into the back of Larcey's throat. Soon he grabbed Larcey's head and held it in place while he pumped in and out. When Little felt like he was about to cum he turned his hind region around and sat on Larcey's face. Larcey attached to the hole like a lamprey, licking and sucking and biting so hard Little wailed and smacked the damp sand around him with open palms. Eventually Little pushed against Larcey's face, signaling the cat to ease up. Larcey took it easy, switching to rimmimg and gentle suckling. Larcey gently sucked at the rim of Little's hole, feeling it flap over into his mouth, combined with the springy nature of the hole, reminding him of a slug.

Then, finally, for the piece de resistance: Little flipped Larcey over completely, tore off the cat's swimming trunks (they were literally in shreds), and aimed his missile-like member at Larcey's anus. Little pounded and pounded Larcey's asshole so hard he thought the cat was going to turn into a puddle dripping off the tip of his dick.

Little pulled the cat's waistline into his own, thrusting his member deep into Larcey's bowels. He pulled apart Larcey's asshole with his fingers so his cock could better slide in and out. The whole time, Larcey bucked and whinnied while Little hollered and slapped Larcey's ass. Finally, shoving Larcey's head into the sand, Little reared black on his hind legs and,

. . . and

Nothing. White. Little doubled over Larcey, exhausted. He was panting. He expected, when he looked down, to see Larcey broken into a million pieces. Instead he saw a word scrawled into the sand:

GORO

"What's that?" Little asked, sweating, panting, pulling on his swimming trunks as he eyed the word written in the sand.

"Oh, that?" Larcey asked, turning to look at the word, slumped over in the sand, looking like he was going to implode in on himself. Larcey grabbed his swimming trunks.

"That word appears every time I cum. Freaky, right?"

Little had crawled away from the word; he was putting on his swimming trunks from a distance. He didn't know what it was but he knew he didn't like it—he didn't like it at all. In fact, he reckoned "Freaky" was a very good word to describe it.

Later that day, as the sun went down, Little and Larcey were walking along the sand when they decided to go surfing. Each of the cats mounted their boards and launched himself into a multicolored bang whizz explosion of lights and sound. Water filled with colors descended upon them, taking them high above the earth. They controlled boards of mass power and superb design, operated only by the most skilled riders: themselves. They broke the laws of speed and sound while barely breaking a sweat. And when they returned to earth, it was as if something precious had been born.

Little and Larcey high-fived.

"Whoa, far-freaking-out, dude!" Larcey exclaimed.

"It was pretty neat, wasn't it," Little said with a wry smile.

Larcey turned to face Little. Slowly, Larcey brought his face to Little's face. He gave Little a peck on the cheek. Little turned to Larcey. He gave him a slow, passionate kiss. By the time it was over, both cats were blushing.

"So I guess I'll . . . see you . . . around then," Larcey sputtered.

It was all Little could do to suppress a giggle.

"Yeah, I guess so, especially since you're part of Sirse's gang or whatever . . . ."

"Yeah," Larcey said. "Or whatever."

The two cats embraced, then kissed. As they turned to part, they touched fingertips briefly in a half handshake, half wave. It made them both laugh. They were gone.

As Little walked home he began to contemplate Sirse again. Why had he ever been suspicious of the cat in the first place? Sure, some weird stuff went down last night, but there was no reason not to trust Sirse, especially since he brought a creature as divine as Larcey into his life. Little started whistling. He held his board high over his head. He was going home, and everything was alright. Better than alright—he had just won the affections of the most gorgeous piece of ass this side of the beach. Thinking about Larcey again—his ripped abs, his tight pecs—Little got a hardon which he juggled, with his surfboard. By the time he reached the end of the beach and had doubled back onto the boardwalk, the sun was going down.

That night, Little was kicking back in his home, smoking weed, when the phone rang. Little froze, holding the smoking bowl in place. He slowly inched a paw over to the phone on the table next to where he was sitting. The noise of the ringing phone pierced the apartment like a police siren. Little let his paw rest atop the phone for one more ring before picking it up.

"Hello?"

"Aye, Little? You there, good buddy?"

Sirse's voice slunk toward him in the dark.

"Yeah Sirse, I'm here."

"Good, good. Because I've got a little job for you tonight, Little . . ."

There was a pause while Sirse chuckle-wheezed at his own joke.

"Yeah," resumed Sirse. "A little job."

"What . . . kind of job?" Little asked.

"Just this thing in the cemetery," Sirse purred.

Little's blood turned to ice.

"Sirse, I don't know if this is such a good idea—"

"You don't know if *what* is such a good idea, Little? You don't know if *what* is such a good idea? You don't even know what the idea is yet. Now—"

Here Sirse took a deep breath. He imagined the cat running a paw over his face, exasperated.

"Can you show up at the cemetery tonight or not?"

Little deliberated for a second, but only a second.

"Aye, Sirse. I'll be there."

"Good. And, uh, bring some rain gear. It's . . . supposed to rain."

Sirse clicked off. Little held the receiver, feeling stupid and alone. A flash of lightning outside. Little stared out the windows. Sirse had been right: It was going to rain.

Four hours later, Little stood in a torrential downpour of rain wearing a slick, plastic yellow raincoat, rubber boots, and a flat-rimmed rubber hat. He held a shovel in one hand as he looked frantically around the cemetery, trying to figure out where Sirse was. It was no use. He couldn't see anything through the heavy rain. As he stood getting soaked, Little gradually abandoned the idea of meeting Sirse here and settled on getting out of this cemetery. But, as if on cue, as Little was searching for a way out, Sirse's Lexus screeched up next to him, crushing headstones and demolishing graves as it did so. Sirse bounded out of the backseat of the car and ran over to Little, where he shook the cat's paw furiously.

"Little, Little, I'm so glad you made it," Sirse said in a slinky, creepy jazz crawl. "And right at the spot in the cemetery I told you to be at! Little, you're one of a kind, you know that?"

Little felt dizzy again. He put the back of his paw to his forehead. He felt like he needed to sit down. He didn't know what Sirse was talking about again (the spot in the cemetery he was supposed to be at?) but he didn't like it. It made him scared and alert. Little's fur stood up on end.

Sirse noticed this.

"Whoa, buddy! There's no reason to get hostile! You're my number one cat, you know?"

Slowly, Sirse lowered his fur to a flattened position. It was true that Little and Sirse had been tight; the closest of acquaintances. Who had set Little up with a free apartment, free *real estate*, when the cat first moved to the beach? Who had provided him with free living wear and other necessary essentials? Most importantly, who had provided him with a brand new board and introduced him to the beach? Sirse had brought Little in with the local group of feline surf denizens and Little knew that no Barter what, even if he could betray everything else, Sirse would never betray the fellowship of surfing cats.

Little nodded.

"Aye, so what do you need Sirse?"

Sirse grinned.

"There you go. I'm glad to see you're finally talking sense."

"Yeah, well, what are friends for?" Sirse said weakly, and shrugged. "Just tell me what you need done."

"Well, Little, I'm just going to need you dig holes in this here cemetery all around the perimeter of this here car—"

Sirse pointed to the Lexus, which, through its high beams, illuminated rain and the graves they fell on.

"—and see if you find anything."

Little paused.

"What kind of . . . thing are you looking for?" Little asked.

"Don't worry, you'll know it when you see it," Sirse growled. "Or, at least, I will, which is why I'm here." Sirse screech-chuckled in a manner evocative of nails on a chalkboard; it caused Little to shudder despite all his efforts not to. But now wasn't the time for thinking, Little knew, so he plunged his shovel into a grave and started digging.

As daybreak arrived, Little thew down his shovel and yawned deeply. Sirse crept up to him from behind his Lexus.

"Hey kid," Sirse purred. "Looks like you did some good work. Too bad we couldn't find what we were looking for . . ."

Sirse had been wondering what they were looking for this whole time; he was too afraid to ask. The cemetery was littered with craters and exhumed graves, but Sirse didn't seem to be interested in any of it.

Sirse waved a paw.

"Alright, let's all just go home," Sirse crooned as he stepped into the backseat of the Lexus. And then as if by magic, the car with the tinted windows swallowed Sirse up and he was gone, propelled into the early morning air.

Tiredly, Little took his rain gear off. The sun was coming up on the horizon and the rain had stopped. Little thought it looked like it would be a beautiful day. He decided to go home, take a shower, get a few hours of rest, and then head to the beach. So he got in his Toyota and drove home.

Later that day, Little was at the beach and feeling fine. The acts of the previous night seemed tame and banal in the fresh beach air. He felt refreshed and reinvigorated, He felt like a new cat. And when he stepped onto that surfboard and into the water, he looked like one, too. He performed some of his most impressive stunts as a surfer yet, riding the water void in all shapes and from all angles, bending the rules of physics, gravity, and geometry as he contorted his body and the water into insane, impossible shapes.

When Little climbed out of the ocean, water dribbling from his mouth, he saw Sirse approaching from a distant spot. Immediately, his belly flopped, but he tried to calm himself. Sirse reached Little's spot on the beach and extended a paw towards the cat. Little accepted it, shook it.

"Hey there, Little," Sirse's voice jazz-pianoed. "I just wanted to say thanks again for last night."

"Oh, no problem, Sire. Any time. I was glad to help," Little said, rubbing the back of his head, feeling his heart begin to pound.

"Well I just want you to know I appreciate it," Sirse said, and began to turn to leave.

"Oh!" Little exclaimed. "I forgot to ask you. How are the sales on the serum?"

"Juicy, junior, real juicy," Sirse chuckled. It was a noise that sent a shiver down Little's spine.

"No sales though," Sirse said, straightening up. "We don't do things like that, you dig?"

Sirse grinned wide.

"Oh yeah, of course Sirse . . . absolutely," Little stammered.

"Good, good, my boy," Sirse said, patting Little's cheeks. "I guess I'll see you around then."

"Okay, Sirse, see you around," Little said, staring as Sirse began to approach the sunset in the distance.

Little sat on the sand, spread his legs, and just sat with his eyes closed for a while. He pinched the bridge of his nose. He saw abstract shapes and black blobs through his eyelids. Then he got up, and resolved to surf away the stress.

Little hit the surf with both feet on his board and his body pressed forward. He wanted to feel every drop of water in the water void while it was still fresh. A mix of color and sound patterns hit him hard, like the journey through space in *2001: A Space Odyssey*. He danced to the rhythm of it all, doing handstands on his board, kicking his feet out in all directions. He navigated his board through water obstacles and optical illusions even a pro surfer would have trouble with. When he washed up on the sand, he felt renewed, refreshed, and reborn.

Sirse's mind was clear. Once again he saw no reason to mistrust Sirse, no ill intentions or shady motives. Everything was at peace because he was a surfing cat on the beach, among a brethren of surfing cats, and nothing could disturb that. So as Little headed for home, he decided to reward himself for his hard work the previous night by checking out some of the beach's night life.

That night, Little hit up a local gay club, Flamingo's. Flamingo's was a nice little place on the beach, two stories with twin balconies; obnoxious music, but where didn't have that these days? Little entered the club with a confidence and swagger that exceeded even his usual self-assured nature.

The owner of Flamingo's and resident DJ was a flamingo perched in the back corner. Flamingo pumped pounding, repetitive trance music throughout Flamingo's.

Little practically traipsed up to the bar, nodded to the bartender. A pint of Guinness was placed in front of him. He nodded to the bartender. Little brought his drink to a quiet corner and watched the theater of the dance floor unfold before him. When someone would stray too far from the center, he might dance with Little, on the periphery, for a brief time. Then the stray cat would reintegrate into his home on the dance floor. This process repeated itself multiple times before Little saw a cat he simply couldn't let go: A drop-dead sexy Tabby, swinging his hips in Little's direction.

The Tabby put his hands behind his head, closed his eyes, and waved his face in the air. He waved his arms in the air, too; and his hands, ears, and whiskers. Little watched the complex interplay of gestures with awe and frank horniness: the cat's erection was now prominently visible through his Bermuda shorts.

When the Tabby tried walking away from Little, Little ran to keep his stride. The Tabby looked at Little, at Little's black and white spotted fur, at his pink nose. Little understood the assessment that was now being conducted, and he hoped the results would be favorable. Finally, the Tabby nodded at Little. Little opened his mouth to say something, but the deafening noise in the club made it impossible to be heard. It didn't Barter at this point, though. At this point, all was decided. The two cats put down their pints and headed out to the street.

Outside, the Tabby got in front of Little again, wandering lost-looking through the night air. Little ran up to him and grabbed him to steady him, thinking him drunk—but the cat remained on two feet perfectly well. Little put an arm around the Tabby's shoulders anyway, for different reasons, and the Tabby responded by reaching over and rubbing Little's chest. The two cats walked this way for a bit, arms tangled around each others' shoulders, hands groping each others' chests. Finally, for the first time in the evening (and Little didn't quite know why it was the first time) Little slipped a finger into the crack of the Tabby's buttocks. The Tabby blushed deeply, but he didn't seem to mind when Little ran the finger beneath his nose. Little offered up the same finger to the Tabby, who rejected it. Instead, the Tabby pulled Little in close and kissed him hard. It continued like this all the way to Little's house.

Once inside the house, Little and the Tabby fumbled their way downstairs to Little's bed. Little wasted no time with foreplay, he pulled the Tabby's trousers off and sat the cat firmly down on his face. Little thrust his tongue into the Tabby's asshole. He nibbled and sucked at the rim of the hole. He felt the springiness of the hole itself with his tongue. He finally turned around and thrust his own asshole in the Tabby's face, burying the Tabby's face, mouth, and tongue in his hole. The Tabby squealed and moaned, accepting the meal with only minor trepidation. For the closing act, Little brought the Tabby gently up from his asshole to his face, kissed him, then turned him around and started pumping his asshole.

Little was lying flat against the Tabby on the bed, making the bed bounce up and down, shake, as he was fucking the Tabby. Finally, he pulled out and ejaculated on the Tabby's chest. When Little finished panting he curled up on his bed. The Tabby curled up next to him, smiling and fingering the tattoo on Little's chest until both cats were asleep.

Little was awake at dawn, watching the early morning light stream into his apartment. On a desk on the other side of the room was a scrap of paper. Little assumed the Tabby had left his number, maybe even his name, before leaving. He threw aside the covers and walked over there to check it out.

Little picked up the scrap of paper and instantly his heart froze. Written on it was the one word:

GORO

Little stumbled back, fell on his bed, and scurried under the cover. He made soft meowing sounds as he tried to make sense of whatever was happening on this cruel summer morning at the beach. Finally, when he felt brave enough, he crawled out from underneath the covers.

Little stood frozen in the middle of the room. The room spiraled around his head like a merry-go-round. Little felt like he was going to be sipped. He dry heaved, swayed towards the bed, then swayed towards the bathroom. He tripped over the phone cord and fell onto beige carpet.

He had tumbled into a hole. There was no bottom.

When Little woke up again it was in a puddle of his own milky white vomit. He could see the sun going down through the windows, which meant it was too late for the beach . . . Though he could still hit the club from last night and try to track down the Tabby. So Little threw some clothes on, jumped in the Toyota, and sped off.

Little arrived at Flamingo's 20 minutes after he left his house, and it was a 30 minute drive, which means he *definitely* broke the law (figuratively speaking; the beach has historically been an anarcho-communist society without any strict laws). Little hopped over the driver's side door and walked up to the club's entrance. This time the bouncer, a tall bulldog, was waiting for him.

"Rawf! What business have you here? Rawf!"

"Calm yourself Bulldog, I wish only to . . ."

Little stopped himself from saying *see the flamingo* and went with "chill out" instead.

"Hmm," the bulldog said, checking the list. "It says here that Little the cat most be barred from the club at all times, but . . ."

"Hey Bulldog, fetch!" Little yelled, extracting a tennis ball from his Bermuda shorts and throwing it into the distance.

Bulldogs have notoriously short attention spans, Little thought to himself and entered the club.

Inside, everything was alive and vibrating with the spirit of bad music played very loudly. The place was packed. Little squeezed himself over to the flamingo in the back corner.

"Flamingo!" Little yelled over the noise of the club. "I need words about a Tabby who was in here last night!"

The flamingo sat frozen in place, perched on one leg, rigid.

"Then how about a word called **GORO**," Little yelled.

This time the flamingo rotated itself, blinked twice, and spoke.

"Sqwuak! What do you know about . . . *that word?*" The Flamingo leered.

"I know it's occurred to me twice after fucking two really hot guys," Little yelled, "And if I ever want to get laid again I should probably figure this out."

"You better be sure you want to know what you want to know," squawked the Flamingo.

Little considered this for a moment, looking at the palms of his front paws.

"Okay, I'm sure," Little said.

The flamingo waved a wing a wall directly to the right of where it was perched crumbled to the ground. Behind the wall was a staircase. No one else in the club was alerted to this: the music was too loud.

Little stared in wonder and amazement down the staircase.

"Well, don't look so shocked," said the Flamingo. "Get down there!"

And the Flamingo kicked Little's rear end, sending him flying down the stairs. At the bottom, Little's head cracked into a wall. He rubbed his aching skull, then struggled to his feet, then wished he hadn't: The Walls were covered in a disgusting slime that stuck to his fur. Little tried licking the slime off his paw but the taste was so powerful it practically knocked him back on his ass. Little kneeled, gagging and hopeless to get the slime off his fur, on the floor of the dark, dank cellar. Finally, he rose, and, having no other option in this lighting, he placed one paw against the wall as he navigated the cellar.

It was nearly impossible to see, but Little could tell by sense that he had just entered a longer corridor, splitting off the one he landed in. He slowly trudged down the corridor, and just when he felt himself on the verge of puking, his feline instincts alerted him to something far more sinister up ahead.

He didn't know what it was, but it smelled like a rotting dumpster. Worse than that. The smell was worse than anything Little had smelled in his whole life. Little approached with eyes squinted, tearing. What was that awful smell? Little walked closer and closer . . . . Until he discovered the reality.

The shriveled up, dried out, mummified husks of a thousand dead cats wandered the walls of this basement. It was unlike anything Little had ever seen. Could have ever imagined. The sheer filth and degradation of the scene was enough to make him vomit . . . four times. Little watched these soulless cat shells wander the floor . . . and then he vomited again. He began shaking as he inched his way further along the corridor, a mixture of fear and revulsion.

The cat husks smelled awful and Little clung to the wall, as far away as he could get from where the cat husks roamed the center hallway. He slowly half-walked, half-crawled down the corridor, further into the darkness.

When Little emerged into light, he found himself staring at his car. He got in. He started driving away from the beach. He never looked back.

Sprawled—part 1

First Circle

The tornado came into my life before I could remember it. Things don't stay pinned down long. It took a long time for me to know the tornado as a thing. Once that happened, it took another long time before I knew it as a thing with significance. Only now am I beginning to gain a sense for what its significance is: Nothing sticks around long.

Now,
before time,
now that I know what time is:
The meaning of the wind and the flying debris.
It has become impossible to ignore.
Nothing sticks around long.

Simon

Bertrand's dad skipped town after he found us making out in the backseat of his Porsche. Bertrand's family, who I'd known since we were kids but not much else except we were poorer than them, never drove that Porsche.

They kept it in the garage with three other cars, an exercise bike, a treadmill, a ping pong table, and cans of gasoline. The gasoline was all we really cared about, besides each others' bodies: We'd huff ourselves into euphoric states before we'd climb into the back of one of the cars and fuck each other senseless. Sometimes we didn't make it onto the backseat.

Generally I fucked Bertrand, but we took turns. The rim of his asshole looked like a curled up slug forming a kind of flap or cleft over the hole. I thought my tight, hairless, pink asshole was objectively better, but he felt good down there. We were usually still giggling when we came, and when I looked in Bertrand's hazel-colored, oval eyes, I was usually seeing literal stars. Those were from the drugs. I was also usually feeling like we were in love. That wasn't from the drugs.

Bertrand had been an intellectual curiosity. In elementary school, a transfer student from England with an accent and hair that was regularly combed, he was insistently polite to our teachers and probably better dressed than the rest of us. We became friends fast, although it was an aloof friendship, his British exoticism pronounced by our dull surroundings. It wasn't until middle school that Bertrand's idiosyncrasies really started to crystallize into something of interest. He stopped being "the weird, chubby British kid" and started being "the weirdly cute, chubby British kid". By high school he had a latent mean streak that some couldn't place but I sniffed out like a drug hound. Bertrand had a caustic wit that was slightly off-putting and a conservative wardrobe of blazers, sweaters, sweater-vests, and slacks. So, basically, just like elementary school, only decidedly fuckable.

When Bertrand and I weren't fucking each others' brains out school was numbing its way through us. He got really good grades, I think because his parents wanted him to go to Harvard because they were rich or something. The details were fuzzy. We didn't talk about it much because we didn't care.

My dad drove a Honda. My mom also drove a Honda. We didn't have a pool. We didn't have a spiral staircase. We were less rich than Daniel's family. Every family in our town seemed to be less rich than Bertrand's family, except the ones that were richer.

It's warm now and I usually walk to school but that day I had the car, so I gave us both rides. My dad's Honda in the driveway must have gave us away. Bertrand's dad opened the garage door to find us having sex, half standing up, Bertrand's hands tense against the Porsche's exterior, my hands tense over his, both of us grinning and drooling. Bertrand's dad screamed some stuff while we both scampered away from him, fumbling around, reaching desperately for our clothes.

I had my shorts and my trousers halfway up as I backed out of the garage. Bertrand was huddling naked in the backseat of the Porsche. I saw terror in his face that I'd never known before. His eyes squeezed tight, face red, the bangs of neatly cut hair trying to say something, hands balled into fists, like the little kid awaiting a beating he'd once been.

I watched Bertrand's fists shake for a second before grabbing my shirt and turning around to get the fuck out of there. That's when I heard a door open and slam and I spun back around. Bertrand's dad was back in the garage, holding a shotgun. He walked over to his Porsche, leaned over and shot Bertrand. Blood plastered the interior. The windows dripped red slime. Then Bertrand's family moved.

Steve

It starts in the dark. I can't make sense of it so here I am, telling it to you. One of us might understand it by the end, or maybe not. Either way I have to try and by the end I'm sure you'll understand why. Okay, ready? Here it goes.

We're speeding through the night in Clayton's car and I'm in the backseat on acid and weed and I'm having an epiphany. I say, "Guys, I'm on acid and weed and I'm having an epiphany." Then I don't say anything. Clayton and Dave laugh from the front and Bart, who's sitting next to me, smiles, I think, although I can't say for sure. The epiphany has something to do with subjectivity and how no one can ever really know anything. Lights are blurry out the window and from the front Dave says something about pickles. Clayton says he doesn't like pickles and Bart agrees.

Clayton tells Dave to call Rohit and Dave says Rohit won't pick up and Clayton says he will and Dave says he won't but he calls anyway. "Yo, brown man, we're headed to the diner . . . be there." Dave snaps his cell shut and says Rohit won't be there. Clayton says he will be there and tells Dave to shut up. I'm watching Bart stare at nothing and then I'm staring at neon zipping past the car. Pretty soon we're at the diner.

At the diner Dave's abusive father is in the parking lot with some other men, which freaks me out more severely than it should. I light a cigarette, leaning against Clayton's car, self-conscious, and then I'm furious at myself and at Dave's dad for making me feel this way so I puff harder on the cigarette and as we walk to the diner's entrance I drop the cigarette and then we all say hi to Dave's dad and I'm pretty sure he ignores us all.

Inside the diner we meet up with Joan and I immediately feel better. She's laughing about a revealing dress she didn't want to wear to an awkward dinner function with Mr. and Mrs. Cooper, David's parents, and I zone out on a Coors Light sign until Andrea, who goes to school with us, takes us to a booth with a stack of menus under one arm.

At the booth Andrea already knows what we want to drink (Joan—chocolate shake; Clayton—grape soda; Dave—water; Bart—lemonade; me—coffee) because we've been there so much, and I'm starting to feel okay with the vibe.

"So," Clayton says. "What now?"

"What now is our salvation," I mutter and Clayton and Bart laugh and Dave mumbles something about how high I am. Bart is talking to Joan about where each of them are thinking about going to college (his top choice: Drew; hers: Lynchburg) which makes me wonder if I'll get into New School, fall in love, and become a successful writer, when all of a sudden I hear what sounds like a glass breaking behind us and then a woman screaming. The woman—probably college-age, blond, thin, hot—has a small piece of glass sticking out of the inside of her elbow which she pushes and twists, and she keeps screaming, and then she's crying, and she drags the glass between a claw, really three shaking fingers, cut up, up and down her forearm, and blood sprays like a drunk kid vomiting a fountain of beer at a fucking party only it's from her goddamn arm and not her face and the blood hits the empty seat across from her and even though she's falling off the plush cushioned booth seat she keeps twisting the glass in her flesh and her skull bounces when she hits the ground.

I look back at Clayton. "What now is we get some beer," I say grinning. Clayton seems to be trying to smile at me but his knuckles are shaking, which isn't a good sign. "I need to go to the bathroom," Dave says, and then he does. Joan is staring at the display of drinks on the wall in front of us. I ask Bart if he wants to go out for a cigarette and he reminds me he doesn't smoke. I get up and walk out of the diner.

Outside the diner door I light a cigarette and look at the moon. Silver smoke hangs in the air and light from the moon shines through it and the clouds look purple in the night sky and leaves on tree branches rustle in the the electric wind and everything is so alive, I can't think of anything ever being more beautiful, and I don't want to.

This is when I freeze in panic because one, two, three, four, five, and then *six* police cars rush into the parking lot, sirens on every single one of them tearing holes in the air, and soon an ambulance rushes in just as fast. Every cop from every car leaves but they're not running after me, they're running into the diner, and then paramedics carrying a stretcher above their heads and attache cases by their sides follow, and pretty soon all of these people are running out, the cops circling the paramedics who are carrying the stretcher only instead of a person being on it there's a body bag with what I'm guessing is a person inside of the body bag on it. I finish the cigarette and walk back inside.

Inside it looks like everybody in the diner is crammed into the vestibule and I crane my neck above people and quickly find my friends and squeeze over to them.

"So . . . uh . . . what's going on?" I say to Clayton.

"We're not allowed to stay in the diner but no one's allowed to leave."

"What the fuck do you mean no one's allowed to leave?"

"I means no one's allowed to leave."

"Fuck this. We're getting out of here."

"No," Clayton says, and his eyes would be telling me something really profound if it Bartered to me at all right now.

"Come on," I say, grabbing his wrist and pulling him; Clayton yanks my arm, pulling me back. I can't resist, so fuck him; I shove my way through fat hot bodies toward the entrance where a cop suddenly leaps at the door, billy club slapping glass, roaring at me, "You're not fucking going anywhere."

Two hours later it's four in the morning and we're finally allowed to leave and everyone is exhausted except me because I'm still on acid. I convince Bart to go to the park with me before he goes home because, I don't know, neither of are exactly in peak mental state, I guess.

At the park we don't say much. There's a huge dick and balls drawn in the wood chips on the playground. Bart decides we should erase them. "Normally I wouldn't care, but I mean, my sister plays here," Bart says. "Yeah," I say, as if this means anything to me. When we're done kicking wood chips over the dick and balls in the wood chips we sit on the swings and start swinging. Some kids approach from behind, laughing. As they pass us they scream things.

"Do you know them?" I say. "No," Bart says. "Just some dumb, drunk high school kids, probably." "Yeah," I say. Pretty soon Bart drives me home and I'm checking the clock on the dashboard but it's all blurry and then I look out the window and the lights from the dashboard and the lights from outside overlap and my head is spinning.

"Uh . . . thanks for . . . driving me home . . ." I manage to say when we get to my house. Bart says something like, "No problem, dude. If I was tripping balls I wouldn't want to drive either," and laughs. I say, "Yeah," and laugh too. Then I say, "See you," and slam the car door.

That brings us here. Back where we started. With me, alone in the dark, typing this all out for you. Like I said I hope you understand why I had to tell it, even if you don't understand it. I mean, I don't understand it, why would *you*? No offense. Whatever.

I sit back and kind of zone out on the screen. School starts in an hour. No way will I sleep. I dig around at the bottom of my underwear drawer until I feel the cold steel box. I wrap my fist around it and make my way downstairs, to the bathroom. One hour until school. I shut the bathroom door, lock it. In the mirror I'm grinning. I guess that means I'm happy. I slide out a razor and do a cut. Sighing I lean back against the sink, letting it bleed. That's better. I turn around and look in the mirror, blood gently flowing from the wound. One hour until school. I'm still grinning. I have a better idea.

Bart

First period gym class is everything gleaming in the sun as it's still rising, reminding you of how it refracts itself through the window in the bathroom when you're showering, how it shines through Jill's fur when you walk her. Pure white light smashes against, jumps back from, the polished bleachers and fences as you finish that lap and kick up dust, and through the dust, as you jog across the field and scare up flying insects, if you look, there's dew on blades of grass, super-green, and it would all be really beautiful if . . . fuck, here comes the ball, and you kick it, and there it goes.

Still, there's satisfaction in the impact, feeling the ball fly in an arc, hit the ground, roll toward the goal, even if it doesn't get there.

You yawn. Breakfast this morning was milk, cereal, toast, butter. Mom running in and out of the kitchen, kind of frantic, as always. Dad in the basement, working on army models. Jill runs up to you and you notice her fur is getting white in places. You pet her and tell her she's a good dog. Sun streams through the window and the particles of dust hang in it as the cereal drops down your throat, making little acidic waves because of the pill, but the pill and the cereal will mix together soon and you'll be here, first period gym class, and the sun won't just be coming through the little window with lilac-printed curtains, it will be everywhere, surrounding you and in your face, and it will be glorious, as you feel wet grass on your ankles, even just for these moments and even if something . . . isn't . . . quite . . . right.

But here comes the ball again, it's back, and you smile and start dribbling it between your feet, up the field, toward the goal. Allison sweeps the ball from between your feet and you grin, you can't help it, and you feel silly in these dumb smelly mesh jerseys that are always too small that they make you wear, but then you're chasing after Allison and it doesn't really Barter.

Daniel is jogging across the field in your direction and you smile at him, say, "Hey," and when he gets to you he's talking about Steve and you remember last night even though you tried to put it out of your mind and Steve's dead. Weird.

Dave

I'm in Home Ec. and pushing needles into my thumb with Andrew. It's just the skin so it doesn't hurt. Pretty funny. From across the room things are shouted and I can't really hear them because they don't Barter. Mrs. Gray is talking loudly about a potluck and I don't know what that is and I laugh as a tiny drop of blood pops up around the latest needle in my finger.

"Check this out."

"Dude," Andrew says, leaning across his sewing machine to take a look.

"Pull that one out of there. You don't want it to actually bleed. Who knows where these things have been."

I have to laugh.

"Yeah man, I know. Isn't it rad?"

Andrew just shakes his head and turns back to his pile of sewing needles.

"Whatever, dude. Just hope that doesn't get infected."

Andrew can be such a fag, it's so weird. Whatever. I push another needle into my thumb, this one gliding easily through the top layer of skin. Lined up with the others it looks great. Perfect symmetry.

"Alright, dipshit? I can do it fine."

Andrew backhands me in the face, waves his needle-thumb at me.

"Don't make me use this," he growls, leering.

"Jesus man! Get the fuck away!"

Big mistake. Mrs. Gray perks up from her seat at the sewing machine across the room, turns from Jessica (hot, big tits), stops talking about "the potluck," starts screaming about "taking the lord's name in vain," threatening to write me up, blah blah blah. Whatever. Everyone is being quiet while she's ranting so I hit the peddle on the sewing machine just to make some noise, which really pisses her off and she sends me to Mr. Achey. Whatever. I pull the needles out of my hand, toss them at the sewing machine as I'm getting up from the desk. Most of them hit the floor. Mrs. Gray doesn't notice, she's already talking to Jessica about potlucks again. I snort and leave the room.

Then as I'm walking down the hallway to the office a girl backs out of a classroom in front of me. She looks like she's been shoved and is about to fall over, but she instantly rights herself, only to collapse forward, the entire momentum of her body hitting the floor. This girl (don't recognize her, younger, maybe a junior) is sprawled on the floor, blocking the entire hallway. She's motionless except her fingers, which are clawing the grout around the bottoms of the lockers that line the hall. I peer down at her, glance into the room she fell out of. No noise. I bend down. Even on her stomach her ass is plump so I slap it hard, getting a boner. I step over her, continue to the office, thinking about that ass in those tight short yellow shorts the whole time. I rub my boner through my jeans pocket, think about stopping into the bathroom to jerk off before I hit the office, then I figure fuck it, I might as well get this over with.

Inside the office is full of commotion and I sigh and slump into a chair to wait for the impending lecture and detentions from Achey. To my left is a fat kid in our grade, don't know his name, think he might be retarded. To his left is Joan and I guess she didn't see me come in because she didn't say anything and I consider saying something but forget it, kicking at the carpet, sighing again, staring at the clock and I can see Joan out of the corner of my eye, playing with her hair, and I'm starting to get a boner again. Joan looks at me and I nod at her and she gets up and I'm drumming the chair's arms with my fingertips and I notice my heart beating but when Joan gets to me she just looks kind of sad and ugly and my heart slows down.

"Hey. What's up?"

"Nothing. Steve's dead."

"What?"

Joan shrugs.

"Steve's dead."

"What?"

Joan shrugs again and then sits back down. I'm leaning around the fat kid to look at her.

"What are you talking about?"

Suddenly Joan gets pissed.

"I'm talking about that he's dead. Okay? Period. End of story."

I stand up. I sit down. I stand up again. I'm sighing repeatedly. One of Achey's secretaries shrieks at me to sit down. I scowl at her and sit. Suddenly an explosion of noise from Achey's office as his mammoth frame fills the doorway.

"DAVID, SIT DOWN. YOU DON'T MOVE UNTIL I'M READY FOR YOU."

Achey turns his back and I flip him off as my eyes drift to the clock and settle there. So Steve's dead. Big fucking deal. Another one bites the dust. Whatever.

Joan

Steve's . . . what, "suicide note"? I guess that's what you'd call it. Anyway, it was in my inbox this morning. It was this long, rambling thing about what happened at the diner and it ended with something like: "I love you. See you in the next life." It was so weird because who leaves suicide notes anymore? I almost felt embarrassed for the poor guy. Then I threw up. Then I felt like punching someone but no one was around so I had to punch myself.

I biked to school with the sun in my eyes. Yeah, he was dead, but so what? The only thing bothering me was the email. Why the fuck would he do something like that? We weren't even such good friends. The more I thought about it the more pissed off I got until I could feel the heat rising in my body and, yeah, it didn't Barter, but I had to tell someone. So when I got to the bike racks, locking my bike up, and Daniel was there too, I said hi and casually mentioned the email. The stupid, selfish email. That was the word for it. Selfish. Daniel agreed that it was selfish, and also weird, and then he mentioned that he had P.E. with Bart this period and he'd pass on the news of Steve's death. Immediately I thought to tell him not to do that, but then I thought, why bother?

Anyway, I felt better after I told Daniel about the email and I could start looking forward to the day being over. But first period was English and Mrs. Farwood sent me to the vice-principal's office for chewing gum. I was pretty relieved to get out of there but I didn't want to face Achey so I took my time on the way to the office. Which was a zoo. Like always. Kids sitting in chairs lined up against the walls all the way from the front of the main office to Achey's private office in the back. There are never enough chairs so a bunch of kids are in the middle of the office just standing around, or sitting on the floor. Like always. Three rows of secretaries behind three huge desks watched over us all. Phones rang constantly and the conversations consisted of whispers and words that no one could hear or, if they could, understand. Like always. I sighed and got in line.

Eventually I got to a seat and tried to let my eyes go blurry on the carpet. It worked until I noticed that Dave was in the office and staring me. Predictably, he looked away, pretending not to see anything. Dave always does that and it makes me so mad. It made me so mad I stood up and told him about Steve right then and there. I don't know why. He deserved it. Even if it doesn't Barter. He deserved it.

Clayton

Algebra II is almost over when I get a text. I wait for Ms. Allen to turn back to the whiteboard before I take out my cell. The text is from Dave.

in trouble with achey. Joan just got yelled at. Wtf. Also She says Steve's dead.

I guess I'm staring at those last two words for too long because the next thing I'm aware of is Ms. Allen yelling at me and I nod and get up from my desk and put my cell away and walk out of the room. I think I'm in trouble and I'm supposed to go to the main office but I go to the bathroom instead and when I get there I have to stare at myself in the mirror for a long time. I don't know how long.

Simon

This was two years ago so death wasn't as normal yet. Nowadays what's the difference. Nowadays, for Bertrand's family is, there probably is no difference. They probably live like nothing ever happened.

I'm sorry, I don't usually get like this. I usually don't think about it. Him. It. Today news of a kid's death leaked and when that happens I can't not. Think about him. Talk about it. Think about him and talk about it. Even though that was then and this was now and that has nothing do with this, what difference does it make if one person dies back *there* and another one dies *over here*, there's no connection and I've been walking down the hall to the bathroom, where I have to take the pill, watching her approach and dreading the moment we will pass by each other because she was his friend and I think her name is

Joan

Pass Simon. He looks totally zonked, as per. Wiping moisture from under my eyes and walking back to Farwood when I see Clayton. He's watching the ground, walking in my direction, and I think about turning around and sprinting in the other direction because that's how tormented he looks, but I wince because he's passing by me in the hall now and I see a face that looks like it's about to fall apart say "Hey, what's up?"

"Nothing" is my reply. Clayton shuffles slightly and I notice he has his arms wrapped around himself and I have to blurt "Clayton, are you okay?" Clayton nods and attempts a smile that makes his face look like even more catastrophic. My feet seem to be stuck in place so I cough and mumble "I guess you heard about Steve." Clayton grimaces and he jerks half of his body away from me. "I have to go see Achey. I'm . . . in trouble." I nod, then notice blood staining the sleeve of his shirt, and a red cut on his arm that the sleeve covers, then uncovers, as he jerks his body. He starts walking away from me.

I inhale hard, eyes closed, rubbing my face the florescent light disappears, no ghostly image or light trails or psychedelic thing or reverse image of your retina, whatever it is when you turn out the lights out really fast and then rub your eyes, you know? There's none of that. Just pitch dark. I have to ball my hands into fists and then I shoot my eyes open at the back of Clayton's neck. "Clayton, we're meeting during lunch." "Uh huh." "Clayton, I mean it. Tell, uh, you know, Dave and everybody." "Yeah," Clayton says, walking away. "We're going to talk about this," I practically shout. Clayton doesn't turn around. I stare at him until he disappears and then I stare at the place in the hall where he disappeared. My pulse is pounding in my temple. I turn and run and start kicking the shit out of the water fountain, wailing, my teeth clenched, or maybe I'm hissing, because I seem to be spitting everywhere, and I'm grabbing the water fountain and shaking it and I can feel the blood in my body rushing forward and back as I try to tear the fucking thing off the wall and I scream and kick it and throw myself into the lockers across from it and I reach into my backpack and with a shaky hand I remove a pill bottle and I drop a pill into my hand and I drop the pill in my mouth and walk back to the water fountain and take a sip.

Dave

It's lunch time.

Shove through tons of fat and ugly people to get to the cafeteria.

It's hard to move. Gross kids are hitting me from all directions, their backpacks clogging the hall, and I'm being sandwiched against a row of blue lockers when I decide fuck this and shove the backpack in front of me, making the kid wearing it double over as it rides up his back to his neck like a turtle's shell, and I laugh and cut my way through the kid and the kids around him, hear someone yell "atom," and I pretend I am one, an atom, pushing and punching and kicking random backpacks and hearing shrieks of surprise and pain as I bounce through the organic Barter around me, the hallway a meat grinder filled with human children waiting to be dumped out the other end, which is the clogged and brightly lit vestibule of the cafeteria, where I arrive, out of breath, laughing.

Adam

I'm walking to the cafeteria and when someone pushes me and I stumble I keep walking. Upstairs in the bathroom the drop is only two flights but it's better than nothing.

There's cracking in my legs and arms when I hit the concrete and blood gets all over my face. I try to move my body but the pain is too much so I stay lying on my back. Wind through the trees makes a strange noise which makes me wonder how hard I hit my head. I carefully rotate my wrist and when the watch tells me it's 11:05 I smile because I've successfully avoided another lunch.

Dave

The giant clock on the wall facing the double doors that serve as the cafeteria's main entrance tell me that it's 11:00 and the sights—emaciated kids sitting or standing around the periphery, tables jammed to twice their maximum capacity as kids literally tumble all over each other and food is spilled everywhere—sicken me with their familiarity until I spot Clayton, Bart, and Joan at the end of a table and make my way over to them.

Joan is covering her head with her hands to avoid being hit by the food or the body parts that are being flung everywhere around her. Fists make contact with the backs of her hands and she turns, barks at the jock next to her, and I smile. Then she turns to Clayton and seems to resume a conversation they were having, and I stop smiling. I pull up a chair next to Clayton, push back against the kids pushing into me with my teeth gritted, then shift my eyes to Joan and say, "Hey."

Joan

I saw Dave enter and immediately lost my appetite. Not that I was eating in the first place. Not that I wanted to eat in the first place. I don't want to be here at all. No shit. I'm here for Clayton. Dave should see that. He should be here for Clayton, too. If he isn't or he can't see that then fuck him, he isn't worth it, and I have no idea why he just sat down next to Clayton and aimed at me a, "Hey."

Dave

I jab a thumb abstractly to the side and follow this up with, "Why do these kids just stand around collapsing into things? Are they too poor to eat?"

"They're not too poor. They just don't eat." Joan says this to me evenly, staring at me, and she's either annoyed or hitting on me but it doesn't which Barter because I'm turned on either way and I notice Tyler sitting in the mass near me but then Bart seems to awake from whatever stupor he was in, turning from a wheat sandwich on a table to ask Clayton, "But seriously, dude, are you okay?"

Bart

You're staring at the peanut butter and jelly sandwich on wheat bread Mom made for you on a darkened table in the dim light of the cafeteria and feeling the impact of kids who play football lunging over each other and hitting you to your right and to your left your friend just sat down next to your other friend. That makes three friends, including the girl sitting next to you,

Joan

Dave just asked an utterly stupid question and I can see this isn't going anywhere and even though Dave has only been here for a minute, tops, I can't fight the urge to bolt but just as I'm about to stand Bart speaks.

Bart

"But, seriously, dude, are you okay?" You ask this and Clayton doesn't say anything, just slumps further into his chair, his gray arms wrapped around himself, projecting a gray aura. You rub your eyes and squint at the florescent lights above you and try to decide if they are the problem or if you are. It has to be the latter. It has to be time to take another pill.

You check the clock. 11:05. Definitely. You gather up a brown paper bag, an uneaten sandwich, a juicebox. You lean across the table to where Clayton is.

"Well, listen buddy, I'm gonna go . . ."

"It's kind of only been five minutes."

It takes you a moment to recover from being startled, but only a moment. It's just Joan.

"Yeah, Joan, I know, but I have to take the pill . . ."

Joan

"Shit. I need to do that too." Suddenly, at the mention of another pill, Clayton's problems get smaller. That's probably mean but so what. Sometimes you have to be mean. The world is mean. Clayton should know that by now. Besides, Dave's already talking to Tyler and they're placing bets on who's going to die next, so I stand up to leave shortly after Bart does.

I place a hand on Clayton's shoulder and bend down to whisper in his ear.

"Clayton, I'll see you after school. My house. Okay?"

Clayton doesn't move or speak, just sits there hugging himself. He's leaning forward on the table and when he lifts his arms I can see new blood stains on the underside of his sleeves.

"Clayton, I need to go to take a pill, but we're hanging after school, okay?"

No response.

"Okay?"

I can't tell if Clayton is recognizing anything I'm saying and, remembering Dave, I turn and shout at him "Dave, go fuck yourself" with the full amount of hostility I can manage before walking out of the cafeteria fast.

I'm walking away from the cafeteria and wiping my face when Dave catches up with me.

"Get the fuck away from me."

"What did I—I just want to—"

"Just get the fuck away," I snarl, and that's when I hear sirens and I look outside and I see Adam, this kid from Home EC, lying on the sidewalk, dripping blood all over, and I suppress a gasp and look into Dave's shallow green eyes to ask, "Clayton takes pills, right?"

Dave doesn't respond and I can't fucking deal with losing it again today so I'm slipping off my bag to fetch a pill of my own as I stare at Dave's blank, dumb face and asking "Dave, Clayton is on pills. Right? Right?"

Circle 2

There have been a lot of them, you know. A lot of boys and girls. They passed through my life. Those are the rules. That's how the tornado works. They passed through my life and sometimes it was my fault and sometimes it wasn't. Whether it was or wasn't, I always blamed myself. That's also how the tornado works.

There's always time for another chance, with another person, in a different place. At least I hope there is. That hope is all I have left. It's like an anchor keeping me from being blown away in the winds. I don't know what will happen if it goes away.

Right now I'm walking to his apartment.

Joan's mom

I woke up. The phone was ringing. I answered the phone. "Hello, Mrs—" The man on the other end mispronounced my last name. "This is Edward Zing from your son or daughters' public school phone alerts system. We just wanted to inform you that a young man, a Mr. Kyle B—" I pulled the receiver away from my ear as this man, this Edward, kept talking. "—obviously nothing to be concerned about, just follow standard procedure in circum—" I hung the phone up. I checked the time. It was 6:00 in the morning. I went back to bed.

I woke up. The alarm clock was ringing. It was 7:00. I pushed off the bed, away from Teddy. I think he was still sleeping. I walked into the bathroom. I turned on the water in the shower. I got in the shower. I took a shower. I turned off the water in the shower. I dried myself on a towel. I put my pajamas back on. I left the bathroom.

Teddy was awake and dressing. I opened the drawers in the dresser we share and dressed with my back to him. I left the room. Teddy was looking at himself in the mirror.

I walked into the kitchen. Joan was standing at the toaster. Nothing was toasting in the toaster. Joan was just standing there. I picked up my wallet from the counter, opened it, removed a twenty dollar bill, and handed it to

Joan. Joan took the money from me. She didn't thank me but she looked overwrought so I didn't say anything.

"Excuse me," I said, and reached across Joan to pick up a loaf of bread. I put two slices of bread in the toaster. Joan slammed a door. The toast was done. I removed the toast from the toaster. I took a knife from a drawer beneath the counter and used the knife to spread butter on my toast. I ate the toast while walking around the kitchen, pouring orange juice and drinking it, flipping through a catalog, watching, through the sliding glass door, the end of summer.

Teddy entered the kitchen and said something. I said something back to him. He left the house. I went back to the bedroom and looked at myself in the mirror. I opened a small round container of cream and wiped it under my eyes, lightly at first and then harder as I worked my way to stretched skin on the sides of my mouth. I'm old.

I left the house. I entered the Toyota. I started the engine in the Toyota and then pulled out of the driveway. I drove to the supermarket. At the supermarket I detached the plastic handle of a shopping cart from the plastic handle of another shopping cart, which was fitted into another plastic handle on another shopping cart, and so on, and I rolled my shopping cart into the supermarket.

Inside the supermarket I took my time shuffling through aisles and picking things up and placing them in my shopping cart. Things I needed: canned corn, fresh corn, potatoes, Hamburger Helper, ground beef, hamburger patties, two bottles of red wine, a 2-liter bottle of Coke, a 2-liter bottle of Sprite, a loaf of white bread, salami, mustard, mayonnaise, peanut butter, jelly, juice boxes, small bags of Frito-Lay chips in one big bag, lettuce, carrots, hot sauce, steak sauce, apples, oranges, gravy.

Things I purchased: canned corn, fresh corn, potatoes, Hamburger Helper, ground beef, hamburger patties, two bottles of red wine, a 2-liter bottle of Coke, a 2-liter bottle of Sprite, a loaf of white bread, salami, mustard, mayonnaise, peanut butter, jelly, juice boxes, small bags of Frito-Lay chips in one big bag, lettuce, carrots, hot sauce, steak sauce, apples, oranges, gravy. I rolled my shopping cart out of the supermarket with these items bagged inside the shopping cart. I wheeled the shopping cart to the Toyota and opened the trunk and took the bags from the shopping cart and placed them in trunk of the Toyota. I wheeled the shopping cart back to the string of shopping carts I had detached it from and placed it back where it belonged. I entered the Toyota and left the parking lot of the supermarket.

I drove home. I opened the trunk of the Toyota. I removed two bags from the trunk and walked to the front door of the house. I placed the bags down at my feet. I unlocked the door and then opened it. I brought the two bags into the kitchen and placed them on the counter. Then I did the same thing with the rest of the bags, two at a time, until they were all in the kitchen.

I was in the kitchen. I started to put the groceries away. I turned on the oven. I filled a pot with water. I placed the pot filled with the water on the stove. I turned on the stove to boil the water. I continued to put the groceries away. I left the Hamburger Helper and three potatoes on the counter. I was finished with putting the groceries away.

I walked into the bedroom. I shut the door. I turned on the television. I lay on the bed. I watched the television for a long time. I got up. I turned the television off. I opened the door. There was mail in the mailbox. I removed the mail. I flipped through it, noticed a routine gag order, and took it with me to the bedroom. I placed the gag order in a cardboard box in the closet. I closed the closet door. I turned around. I looked at myself in the mirror. I left the bedroom.

I walked into the kitchen. I removed a potato peeler from a drawer beneath the kitchen counter. I began to peel a potato. After the potato was peeled I dropped it into the pot of boiling water on the stove. I picked up another potato and began to peel that one.

The front door open. Joan entered, followed by three of her friends. One of them looked unusually terrible but I tried not to think, turning back to the potato. I continued to peel the potato. I finished peeling the potato and dropped it into the pot of boiling water. I picked up a third potato. Joan entered the kitchen. She was carrying a gray flannel shirt, sleeves of which were covered in blood.

"What the hell," was all I could say to Joan.

"Just get rid of this," she snapped.

I put the potato down. I took the shirt from Joan. She turned and left the kitchen. I stood in the kitchen. I walked to the bedroom. I placed the shirt in the cardboard box in the closet. I closed the closet door. I left the bedroom and as I was walking back to the kitchen I heard loud voices from Joan's bedroom across the hall and glanced in to see Clayton wearing a flamboyant purple blouse.

Clayton

Monday
It was circulating forever but it crystallized, for the last time, after school that day at Joan's house. I knew there was nothing these people could offer me but, burning alive, I

52

went anyway. I arrived and my worst fears were confirmed: Glancing across a gathering of faces I loathed, didn't know anymore, never knew, or a combination of the three—Joan, Dave, Bart—I was never more detached from everyone and everything.

Let's pause here to note that these are not the principle figures in our tale—far from it. My sister, my mother, my brother, my town, Dave's parents who he openly chats with about his perception of my drug use—all part of the never ending weight that led to this moment.

I choked down panic attacks the entire night. Until I finally left after sitting in an underwater bubble, staring at a corner, not part of myself, any self, or any world.

I would say that day was the most depressed I've ever been, but that wouldn't be giving enough credit to the days that followed.

Joan's mom

So it must have been his shirt I was to get rid of. Was he gay now or something? I tried not to think about this and I walked back to the kitchen where I finished peeling the third potato. I dropped the potato into the pot. I placed the lid on the pot. The potatoes boiled. I watched steam leave the pot where the lid was ajar. I left the kitchen.

I walked back the bedroom and the voices from Joan's room were quieter than before. I opened the closet. I opened the closet. I stared at the cardboard box. I closed the closet door. I sat on the edge of the bed. I watched the television even though it was off. I heard the front door open. Teddy walked into the room. He was holding mail. He didn't say anything.

I walked to the closet. I opened the door. I gestured at the cardboard box.

"You need to burn these things," I said to Teddy. He grunted.

Joan's dad

I picked up the cardboard box that was in the closet. It was not heavy. I left the room. I walked downstairs and peered into Joan's room and saw that she was sitting in there with three boys, although one of them looked like a total queer, which was somewhat of a relief. I left the house through the backdoor, into the backyard, and I kept walking into the woods behind the house.

I lit a fire in the fire pit and removed an item from the box. A shirt, which I saw in the glow of the fire had blood all over it. Appalled, I threw the shirt into the flames, thinking AIDS, rubbing my hands vigorously on my pants. I noticed that I had not been given the opportunity to change into jeans when I got home and cursed my wife. I watched the flames eat the shirt and then removed the letter from the cardboard box. Another gag order. I opened it. ". . . aware of the death of student Kyle . . . ." I scanned to the bottom of the letter for the predictable ". . . legally required to burn this notice after . . ." I tossed the letter into the fire, and then the envelope. They burned fast. The shirt took longer to burn. I wondered what it was doing in there and then tried not to think about it. The flames died down and I filled a bucket with water and poured it over the pit, smothering what was left of the fire. My wife was standing at the backdoor of the house and shouting at me that dinner was ready and I grinned painfully, wanting to hurt her. I walked into the house and sat at the table.

Joan's mom

I prepared the hamburger helper while Teddy burned the items from the box. The hamburger helper was finished and I set the table. I placed three plates on the table. I placed three napkins on the table. I placed three sets of forks and knives on the three napkins on the table. I placed three glasses on the table. I poured two glasses of red wine and set them on the table. A 2-liter bottle of Coke and a 2-liter bottle of Sprite sat in the middle of the table. I served everyone. I walked to the backdoor and shouted to Teddy that dinner was served. He didn't say anything. I told Joan that dinner was ready and she told me to get away from her room. I walked back to the kitchen. I heard three people leave the house. Joan entered the kitchen. She sat in front of her food at the head of the table and didn't say anything. Her father entered the kitchen from backyard and sat at the table. I sat at the table. Joan's father downed the glass of wine and smacked his lips. "More?" I asked him. He didn't say anything. He picked up a fork and was shoveling the potatoes I made and the Hamburger Helper I made into his mouth. Joan picked up her fork and stabbed at the potatoes on her plate. I turned to Teddy and asked, "How is it?" He didn't say anything. I tried again. "How was work?" He didn't say anything. I looked at Joan, who had her head down, pretending to study the food she wasn't eating, and I asked her, "How was school, honey?" Joan gave me a look that was so hateful I never wanted to ask her anything again. We ate.

After dinner I cleaned plates and the forks and the glasses and placed them in the dishwasher. I turned on the dishwasher. I walked to my bedroom where Teddy was lying on the bed, wearing heavily stained briefs and no shirt. I looked at myself in the mirror. I unscrewed a lid from a small round container and rubbed cream on my face and neck. I walked into the bathroom. I flossed and brushed my teeth. I left the bathroom.

I watched Teddy on the bed, watching television. I asked him, "How was work?" He didn't say anything for a while and then he said, "Shut up." I looked at the television and saw corpses decorating a nightclub on the news. "What are you watching?" I asked Teddy. He farted and turned his back to me. I got in bed next to him and closed my eyes. I slept.

Joan's dad

I woke up. The phone was ringing. I slept.

I woke up. The alarm clock was ringing. It was 7:00. I pushed off the bed, away from my wife, then I noticed she was in the bathroom. Relieved, I stuck my hands in my briefs and started scratching and rubbing my balls. I removed my hand from my briefs, sniffed it, farted. I rested my face in my hands and rubbed my eyes, still enjoying the piquant odor from my balls. I farted again.

I stood up. I hobbled over the closet. I am getting fat. I did not have time for a shower because my bitch wife always gets up too early and takes the bathroom from me so I removed a pair of slacks and a shirt from their place in the closet and began to put them on. My wife exited the bathroom and I walked to the mirror, avoiding her. She left the room and I got angry, then I forgot about it. I walked back to the closet. I removed a tie. I tied the tie around my neck in front of the mirror. I walked into the bedroom, my slacks pulled down around my thighs, and sat on the toilet. I closed my eyes and shit. I opened my eyes and wiped myself. I rinsed my hands and walked back into the bedroom. I tucked my shirt into my slacks. I pulled up my slacks. I put on a belt. I left the bedroom.

I walked downstairs. I did not want to acknowledge my wife or Joan, who were in the kitchen, but I had to retrieve my car keys. I walked into the kitchen. I picked up my car keys. My wife said something.

"What?" I said.

"What?" she said. I looked at her.

"Oh," she said. Thankfully, Joan ignored me. I left the kitchen.

I left the house. I entered the Nissan. I started the engine in the Nissan. I tuned the radio station to WBGO, the local jazz station. I hummed along to songs as I drove to work. There was minor traffic and I only swore and honked a reasonable amount.

At the office I screeched the Nissan into a parking space. The office is a MetLife building where I work. I glanced at the nets hanging below the roof as I walked into the building.

I sat at a desk. For four hours I entered data into a computer screen. Then I went to lunch with another guy from IT. At lunch I had a drink and a terrible burger. After lunch we went back to the office.

I sat a desk. For four hours I entered data into a computer screen. Then I left the office and entered the Nissan.

I started the engine in the Nissan and pulled out of the parking space. I tried to hum along to WBGO but as I approached the house I couldn't focus. I felt my blood pressure rising. I wanted something. I didn't know what it was.

At the house I parked the Nissan in the driveway. I slammed the car door. I entered the house. I slammed the door of the house. I grabbed the stack of mail on the coffee table in the living room. I walked upstairs. Joan was in her room with three boys, one of them a faggot, thank God. I walked into the bedroom. I saw my wife and I wanted to kill her. She was talking about some things in a box that needed burning. I grabbed the box and slammed the door of the bedroom as I left it. I burned the things outside. I considered beating the shit out of my wife and laughed. My wife told me dinner was ready. I ate dinner fast, burped, and walked upstairs to the bedroom. Exhausted, I took off my clothes and got into bed. I flipped on the television. CNN showed some kind of suicide party, dead kids, more of the same. When my wife entered the bedroom I turned because I couldn't bear to look at her. I pretended she was dead. I slept.

Dave's dad

I woke up. The phone was ringing but Deborah seemed to be attending to it. I couldn't sleep again and I felt my pulse rise in my body fast and I shoved Deborah hard and she got up and left the room. At 7:00 I walked into the bathroom. I shit. I showered.

I left the bathroom. I took a sip from the flask. I took another sip. Walking through the kitchen to leave the house and go to work I grabbed Deborah and kissed her hard. She seemed to be resisting so I kissed her harder until she relented. I released her and left the house.

I got in the piece of shit Previa and started the engine. I pulled out of the driveway. There was a new construction site that needed my attention. I checked the printed map for directions and started to drive there.

On the way there was a huge traffic jam and I lost it, rolling down the windows and to scream and curse at everyone, holding the horn, shouting and spitting into the morning air, jerking in my seat so hard the car shook. Panting, out of breath, I took a long sip from the flask and wiped my mouth. I stared straight ahead.

The construction site was not interesting, just stupid people doing their jobs poorly. I finished the flask there and didn't have enough for the drive home. On the drive home I cursed myself furiously.

At home I poured myself a drink and sat at the kitchen table. Richard entered the house. I smacked him in the face promptly.

"Dad," Richard said.

I smacked him again. Blood spurted from his nose. I felt better.

"Dad," Richard said, although he was holding a sleeve to his face and his voice was muffled in a way that made me laugh. "Dad," he sputtered again. "Why?"

"Because it's . . . 7:10" I said, glancing at the nearest clock. "You're late for dinner."

"Dad, we never eat dinner together," Richard said patiently. "I was just at Joan's house. I left when her family was having dinner."

I threw the glass into the nearest wall. "I don't care about that whore! Ge the fuck back here!" Richard is running now, trying to get upstairs "Don't say we never eat together! How dare you disrespect your mother like that? Do you know how much work—" But Richard is gone, and it's too much work to chase after him. I sigh and sit back down. I stand up. I grab the bottle of Jack. I sit down. I drink.

Clayton's shrink

"Than you, Dr. Truth."

I smile curtly and hand Kurt his script for the cure.

"If that doesn't work . . . Well, it will work. If it doesn't we can up the dose."

Kurt nods and leaves the office. I lean into the waiting room. About twenty kids lined up. The line snakes around the waiting area but doesn't double back on itself. Not a bad afternoon.

"Next?"

A young man who I recognize but whose name escapes me enters the office. Embarrassed, I flip through the numbered flash cards for the two hundred patients I see each day. I arrive on the proper card. "Hello, Clayton" I say warmly. "Hi," Clayton says coldly. I furrow my brow, annoyed by his snippiness. He is in the chair across from me. "So what's been going on?" "I don't know." I furrow my brow, annoyed by his snippiness. I look at flash card. "You're not taking the cure?" I ask surprised, noting how thin he is.

"No . . . but I don't think it Barters—"

"Of course it Barters," I say, cutting him off. "I don't know why you weren't on it already. There must have been a terrible oversight. I'm sorry."

"No, it's fine. It's just that my best friend, uh, he—"

"It's okay," I say firmly, sensing the necessity of moving away from this subject. "Let me just write you a script. What's your height and weight?"

"Please, uh, Dr. Truth? Can we just talk about my—"

"Please, Clayton. Can you just tell me your height and weight? Oh, it doesn't Barter. We'll start you off at four pills a day. We can up the dose if it isn't effective." I rip the script from the pad I've been scribbling on and offer it to the patient across the desk. "Okay?"

The patient takes the script, mumbles something I can't hear, and leaves the office. I sigh heavily. That was a close one. Weird that he wasn't on the pill yet. Weird that he wanted to talk. I shake my head, stand up, take a deep breath, clench my buttocks for ten seconds, and sit back down.

I lean into the waiting area.

"Next?"

Clayton

Tuesday

I slept a reasonable length for the first time in days. Head mostly clear of the after effects of Kyle's suicide, I felt physically well enough to go to school without puking before or during, although the cuts on my arms were making that hard. After school I went to my psychiatrist for the first time in I don't know how long. Brad wasn't there. The good news: None. Either while this was happening or shortly after, or shortly before, or all three, I started thinking about Kyle again.

The man who broke my heart? I mean, why am I reacting this way now? I know people who have died. We all do. Would I feel this way if it had been Joan, or Dave, or Bart? I hate asking that, I feel so guilty, but I have to. I don't know why. Something had been building, and I guess that was the break, the snap, the release.

The man who broke my heart represented an entire group of people, an entire reality, the possibility of reconciliation with that reality, breaking my heart.

The problem was, I couldn't get out of there. The idea of Brad as a gateway to another reality stopped me from going under completely, but I knew how distant that was and always would be.

Meanwhile, Kyle had killed himself. Everyone was a drug addict. I was about to be a drug addict too because my shrink just prescribed me the cure. The idea of death was very, very sexy.

Meanwhile, I was left twisted and distorted, one world eating me like a cancer and the other unattainable. I was nobody to anyone, most of all myself.

That night I called Dave and told him how I thought Kyle broke my heart while I cried. He called me a fag. I called him a cunt and stuff.

Clayton's mom

I'm home from dinner with Bret. He didn't say much and I didn't want him to. I asked him about alimony. I asked him why the child support was late. He slammed his fist on the table. I smiled, not having to deal with him any more.

Before that I saw my shrink. Oh, I think Clayton was supposed to see his shrink today. I hope he did. I jangle my keys from where I sit in the car, watching the house. There are no lights on. It's late. I hope Clayton is home. I don't want to go in there though.

Anyway, the shrink said they doesn't usually prescribe the cure for adults, but I could have it if I really wanted it. I said I'd think about it. I am thinking about it. I really want it.

Before that was work. Being a high school teacher is hard these days. Seven students were absent from my classes. Fifty were absent from the school in total. I rub my eyes thinking about this.

We get the gag orders and then burn them. We are legally required to read and then burn these letters that come every morning and that list the "casualites," as the government calls them, even though we don't what is happening or why. We just know that our children are dying.

Before that I left for work while Clayton was still asleep, or else he had left already. Anyway, he wasn't around. He never is in the morning. I look at the house. I'd like to spend more time with him but it just isn't possible these days. He's getting older. I am too. I look at all the dark windows in the house. I don't want to go in there.

Clayton

Wednesday

I didn't take the pill because I didn't see my mother yesterday so I couldn't give her the prescription to have it filled. I apologized to Dave in a text, told him we should chill after school. Really I just wanted to talk about my feelings about all this—I had no intention of chilling with him. No response from Dave. I quickly unapologized in a string of well-placed obscenities while I asked Joan what was up. She said Dave was saying I was being weird and we definitely all needed to hang out after school.

63

After school I slept. I was probably dead already, at that point. I drove to Burger King.

I asked Joe for the gun.

I asked Brad if he wanted to hang.

Two ways of departing a life that had been intolerable for too long.

No response from Brad.

A response from Joe.

I thought about things and then slept.

Bart's mom

It's a gorgeous day and I just took Jill for a walk. Now I'm putting the finishing touches on a casserole for dinner. Bart should be back from school soon. The classic rock station is on and I'm humming along to a song I recognize while sun pours into the kitchen, warming my hands at the sink below the window. It's a gorgeous day.

"Honey?"

Bart's dad

Beatrice calls to me from upstairs and I smile. It's nice to hear her voice. I place the antique revolver carefully on the work bench.

"Yeah?"

Bart's mom

Thomas calls to me from downstairs and I smile. It's nice to hear his voice.

"I need another pill."

Bart's dad

"Okay. I'll bring it up to you in a minute."

Bart's mom

"It's okay, I'll just come downstairs." I smile again, turn around in the kitchen, swing my skirts like a ballerina, like I'm young again. I let the sun bathe my face. I walk downstairs.

The basement is filled with old US Army antiques. I don't know the names of nearly all the things down here but there are a lot of old bullets and artillery shells and guns. There's even a tank in one corner. I make my way over there because that's where Thomas is. He's leaning against a bookcase behind the tank and the big round glasses he's wearing make his eyes even more full and warm and when I look at his cropped auburn hair, graying only on one side, I still recognize the man I married.

Thomas looks at me, smiles, and gives me a big hug. I hug him back and bury my face in his neck. He smells like pine. "You wanted the cure?" He asks, playing coy. "Mhmm," I say, playing right back, making eyes at him. He grins. "You got it, babe." He removes a book from a shelf and takes the bottle of pills from their hiding place. He studies the label purposefully. "Hmm, only for Bart . . ." I laugh, throwing my head back. "I think we can break those rules though." He winks at me. I giggle and bite my lower lip. Thomas walks toward me and slips a pill between my lips. He smiles and raises a glass of wine from the shelf behind him. He tilts the glass of wine at my lips and I sip through a grin. He takes the glass from my hand and I stare at him as he pops a pill and downs it with the wine. I grab back the wine, spilling red on my hands, and pop another pill. I giggle. He's staring at me. I run upstairs and lock the door.

Bart's dad

We're eating dinner with Bart's friend, Clayton. He looks sick. He looks like he's lost twenty, maybe forty pounds since I last saw him. He looks gaunt. He also keeps rubbing his arms under his flannel shirt like he's hiding something.

"So, Clayton, how's your mom doing?"

Clayton shrugs, doesn't look up. I hope he isn't a junkie or something. Beatrice is looking at him with vague panic. I sigh. You can't save them all. Beatrice should know that.

Clayton

Thursday

I sent Dave a vicious text as soon as I woke up. I asked Joe more info about the gun. Eventually I got more info about the gun. It all seemed confirmed at this point.

During school I got a call from a number I didn't recognize and, alarmed, I didn't answer it. After a few minutes I called back with my number blocked. It was Bart. I didn't have his number for some reason. I was relieved. He wanted to know if I wanted to come over to his house after school, maybe stay for dinner, and even though I was planning to go to bed after school I said, "Okay."

I met up with Bart during lunch. I was wearing a WHY? Shirt. Bart recognized the band. For a moment or two I felt connected to something. On the way to his house, after school, we pumped "Crushed Bones".

After I left Bart's house I drove around alone, pumped WHY?, felt connected to the idea of myself as a "self," but not really feeling anything.

So now I sit here, in my room. I don't know where my mother is. I'm waiting for Joe to get off work and text me about the gun. Tomorrow is Friday. By the time you read this, I'll be dead.

Achey

I undo a belt buckle as fire blazes in a portable fire pit on top of my desk. The flames are huge. We had a lot of paperwork today.

The office is empty except for me and I let the flames warm my face in the dark. Smoke rushes up and out the chimneys that have been installed above every secretarial desk. One-third of the student population has been reported dead or missing, and the first month of school isn't even over yet. Sometimes I have to wonder if the government really has this under control, but I don't have to wonder long. I have to try not to think about it.

I slap my belly. I am fat and old. I squint into the flames before me. I sniff. I have to wonder about Kevin, though.

I Hate to Eat and Run

"I hate to be alive," he says, "but I have a social responsibility to attend to."

He looks up.

Nurses asking how he's feeling. A strained, automatic reply. Nausea rips through his stomach. No, don't think about that. You're here now. This is all that matters.

Fireflies dancing in the bruised sky. Light from lamps trickles down to the street. She's out there, somewhere in the distance. He's sitting behind her, then he's shoveling her food into his mouth, sucking on it, while she pulls away in shock and horror and others laugh or get up or just sit there, but knowing.

Is this how you flirt? Head in hand, hunched over a notebook on a bed, writing like this is all that's left, like is all that matters, anymore, will this make sense someday? Should I kill myself? Years of aging, heading to no certain future. What future is? Right, but I'm not *looking forward* to it. Minimal hope, minimal things to care about. Am I going to kill myself yet?

"That doesn't even make sense," she says, and sneers at the ground. Spaghetti. Plates flying and then crashing. A tightening in my chest. Just get through this, I think. Just this one.

He's sitting on a swingset, kicking dirt and watching the ground as he swings back and forth. Fuck, he thinks, am I really still free? How much longer will this go on? "When do we leave?" he asks her, and smiles. He looks down when he smiles. She keeps staring at him and when she reaches to take his hand it's gone, a miniature black hole on a stump at the end of his arm. She screams as her hand is sucked into his.

Why is This Country Such a Catastrophe, I thought To Myself and as Ususal No Answers Came Even Though I Felt I Knew Them All Already.

Why is This Country Such a Catastrophe, I thought To Myself And as Usual No Answers Came Even Though I Felt I Knew Them All Already. I punched some words into a keyboard. *That's Probably Because You're Avoiding The Question That Matters with The One That Doesn't.* I imagined these words, chewing the eraser-end of an imaginary pencil. I punched more words into a keyboard.

The police detective seemed like an alright guy. I wanted him sexually, or like a child would his father, or both of those things. These feelings are becoming blurry to me.

Everything is becoming blurry. Tightened dread begins to recoil as one more cop passes through my life, the encounter another bowel movement—another meal, in my case, because I enjoy shitting more than I do eating, and I don't exactly enjoy either—or not, because it might build to something. Something about the detective made me think this wouldn't be a thing that builds to something, it would be a thing that takes things away. It won't be. One has to consider the circumstances I'm already living in to appreciate the reality (admittedly hard for everyone, expect, seemingly, myself): whether I was actually anti-disgusted by this cop or not, the experience will be passive-aggressive invisibly contextualized into one more isolating brick of failure in the matrix of shame that separates me from my family on every psychological level a person has a name for.

Time to slow down?

I punch some more words into a keyboard. Things feel like nothing. "Punch" is hardly an exaggeration; I'm slapping these keys like the motherfuckers they are. Like the motherfucker I am. I ponder that for a moment. No use. *Why Is This County Such A Catastrophe*, I thought To Myself And As Usual No Answers Came Even Though I Felt I Knew Them All Already.

It's The End of The World
and I Don't Know How I Feel

To Joan Didion, for "Slouching Towards Bethlehem"

The center is not holding—maybe for real this time. We joke about the end of the world, in the dark, in the cold, with power lines torn down and trees snapped at the root. These block roads. Houses are all black.

I do not mean to suggest that our (perhaps) "minor" (it is impossible to know the extent of the damage at this point, because we have no electricity or means of hearing news from the outside world (if that news could even be trusted)) October Ice Age is some unprecedented weather-related catastrophe on scale with, say, New Orleans (although it is already obviously more significant than the pitiful non-event Hurricane Irene from a few months ago). All I am suggesting is that it is a major sign of the end of the 21st Century. 1 hour remains.

They stole Halloween. The bastards.

We were acting like characters from that Joaquin Phoenix "documentary". We were pretty fucking stoned. I make no apologizes for what this is. It's a diary of the apocalypse, real or imagined. Something sinister is happening.

We're bracing ourselves for the end of the world now. I am. Sitting here, watching *Lost Highway* on what's left of my laptop's battery and not paying attention, thinking instead about the girl I lost on purpose, the girl I lost by accident, the girls I may never know.

"We're all wired into a survival trip now," to quote Hunter S. Thompson. At least that's what it feels like. In the cold, and the dark, the only sound that can be heard are store-bought power generators in the distance (and how long can they last?). The cars that still work disregard the police barriers outright, not that it matters because a) no one's around to enforce anything and b) the barriers are useless because the cars can't get anywhere anyhow. The cars seem to know this but they inch along the ice roads anyway, the need to know what's going on more powerful than the need to actually get anywhere. Where is there to go? The town is bankrupt (not to mention the state and country). The police—busy placing wooden roadblocks that will soon be swept away in gusts of wind or, if not, completely ignored—are completely powerless and this would probably be funny (well, funnier) if the entire context didn't already feel like a cruel joke. To say that law enforcement is non-existent is not an exaggeration. Traffic lights don't work and if you feel like driving through the arctic jungle this place has become you'll notice that everybody seems to be floating by on the ingrained rhythms of the daily routine, but how long will this numbed peace last? There seems to be some shared, silent understanding of this, whispered in the shadowy corners of the adult world while the facade of business as usual—the collection of storefronts at the town's center—continues to shine through the frost, half-bright. The kids who aren't towing the party line talk about it openly—this is it, the end of the world—and we joke about it, and make movies about it, and predict how long until things get *really* bad. I'm one of them (I'm writing this, after all), but I don't know how I feel. It's the end of the world, and I don't know how I feel.

Uncontrollable fit of shaking. I am in the dark in the coldest part of the house. That is, my bedroom. I fear I am going to die.

The shared thought (at least among those of us who care about such things) looming over all of this, the one we have no answer to—What happened to Wall Street? Who did this?

"He's either dead, high, or working on some insane art project. Maybe all three."

"It's some seriously prophetic shit."

"If you ask me another question, I'm going to slit your fucking throat."

These are all spoken, thought, or written on November 1, 2011, the day after the end of the world.

Starbucks—we joke about how we're bringing in a MacBook Pro and bottled water, but do we have a choice?

On the fifth day it was noticeably warmer outside than it was inside, so I went out into the not-as-freezing sun and read on the front steps of the house. I can't remember the last time I did that.

In the pitch black of frozen backyards and parking lots I made myself throw up a bunch of times. In a speeding car on an empty highway I gave myself cigarette burns and wailed in pain in between hooting out lyrics to Strokes songs. I did these things because I had nothing else to do. Then I wrote them down in a notebook. Imagine that.

We saw *The Rum Diary* and my mind looped on a few thoughts: *This is nothing like the book*; *Where are the drugs?*; *This movie sucks; I want a cigarette.* I left him for a cigarette and stayed for two, singing Kanye lyrics and barely lowering my voice to say "nigga" because the parking lot was black and empty. I could have been jumped at any moment (quite easily—I don't think I could see more than two feet in front of me in any direction), but at the time I figured that would be a beautiful death. I considered ducking behind a shrub and smoking a bowl.

We drove for no reason other than that we didn't want to return to our former homes, with the windows down and music blasting. He obeyed traffic laws more or less like he always did, stopping for the odd traffic light that still worked, but for what reason? Who was around to enforce these laws? What laws were even in effect? Why didn't we try to find out? Are we really so trapped that even when our beautiful, dark, twisted, anarchist fantasy comes true (it's not really any of those things, I guess, except dark), we can't seize its reigns? I ask these questions not just out of rhetorical affect but because I genuinely don't know the answers to them.

In the absence of law enforcement we pretended to be cops for a little bit. It felt dirty.

I constantly wanted ecstasy. I thought about robotripping more than once but never did, knowing where that would lead.

Powerlines cracked to splinters at their crossed masts. A giant cross (not a powerline) blocks the road like death. That was the most blatantly ominous image of all. For a while there, on the first day, I thought I'd somehow end up dead on it like Donnie Darko.

When I saw myself in reflections I desperately wanted to shave, self-consciously touching the hair on my face. I looked too much like a Man—the most dreadful and evil of all animals.

At this point, in my mind, one thing reverberated above all else and that was: *Get out. Do whatever you have to, just get out of here and go. This place is finished.* At this point, though, is there even time left for that? It feels like choosing which vantage point you want to watch the apocalypse from. Right now, any life choice just feels like choosing the position from which you are going to watch the whole thing collapse.

In lieu of TV news we decided to make our own news, at least while the batteries in our camera lasted. He was the cameraman and I was the gonzo journalist. We agreed that every time I signed off, illuminated in the pitch black by the camera's night vision function, I would say, "Welcome to the apocalypse". I said it when we turned the camera on, as well—it was my greeting and my farewell. There are no more "goodnights" and no more "good lucks". Welcome to the apocalypse.

As the snow starts to melt and the hum of the electric generators is audible and I realize I'll probably be typing this soon, I also realize it was as much for him as it was for me. His entry-level job is killing him, he constantly tells me—killing his sex drive, killing his dreams, killing everything. I empathize with him, even though at this point I should know better and in fact see my incessant, extreme empathy for everyone and everything that hurts as the single biggest affliction on my life. Would I be writing this without it? I don't care. I still don't like to see people in pain. At this point I should just leave every single one of them behind and never look back. Every single one.

In a bookstore I flipped through Frank Miller's *Holy Terror*. I've always known Miller admired the people he writes about, but that didn't make me want to set the book on fire any less (Would anyone have noticed? Cared? I was pretty sure law enforcement was still utterly crippled, but who could be sure).

I guess we basically did what we always do. Only this time it was the apocalypse.

There is a part of this story I'm leaving out, partially because I'm trying to leave it out of memory. It involves an apartment rented by a man who ruined my life, who continues to ruin my life. The memory of this man and his continued existence in this mortal realm haunts me daily. Not a word of that is exaggeration. I'm not going to say anything else.

Or, well, I wasn't planning to. But then this happened:

I dreamed of Samantha (or, rather, a Samantha simulacrum) and woke to my brother telling me to give him a ride someplace. I didn't want to leave her but, having no choice, threw my sleeping bag to the side. The romantic dream was replaced by the bitter reality that Samantha is dead because she killed herself as I drove my brother to the place. "Bitter" seems like a good word for it, because it stung. Writing that, it still does. I was reminded of a fairly simple idea for a detective story about a private eye and a teen boy whose girlfriend committed suicide, only she didn't commit suicide, she was murdered. The idea for the story came to me (when else?) around the time of Samantha's death and I haven't written it for the same reason I am writing this now. That reason comes back to a question I asked myself last week: "How do you write about the apocalypse from inside of it?" Samantha's death still hurts too much to do anything with it, and I've always lived life through the written word, so maybe that's why it still hurts so much? This apocalypse, in contrast . . . I don't know. It's the end of the world and I don't know how I feel.

Anyway, being reminded of Samantha's suicide left me pretty steamed, so I drove around fast, disregarding traffic laws, flipping off soccer moms, changing lanes at mach speed until I crashed into the back of an SUV. The driver of the SUV made a sharp right and pulled over, expecting me to do the same. The chump.

"Just Go. Go. Go. Go." I screamed at myself as I attempted to flee the scene, only to find that I'd completely fucked up my car's steering. Still, I managed to navigate my way out of there without further incident, swerving up and then back down an endless series of cordoned off streets, gripping the wheel like it was a bar of soap the whole time. For all I know the weasels could be out looking for my plates right now. Unlikely, though—chaos, apparently, still reigns.

How many suicides have I inadvertently help cause? One that I know of. I'm sorry, Sam.

I have to get out of here, although "I have to get out of here" is becoming an increasingly farflung, even callow, sentiment. A more apt one might be the question, "What am I going to do?" Grow up.

Or maybe I'll just give myself another cigarette burn or three and drift somewhere in my mind. This is getting maudlin.

for all the gifts god's blessed me with
she's thick as shit

I pull on a tie-dyed shirt with even more irony than usual. A Halloween decoration from back in the 21st Century—a skeleton in parody of a hippie: shock of dyed hair, Mardi Gras beads, AC [lighting blot] DC shirt (I scoff at the anachronism), flashing the peace sign, its arms snapped off, a plastic skeletal "peace" hand lying in the gutter, covered in frost.

The car was only operable with the steering wheel twisted completely on its side, which was kind of cool, but, not wanting to fuck up the car even worse, I took it easy getting here, and the only reason I left at all is because staying would mean being completely blocked into the house by emergency vehicles, repair vehicles, and law enforcement vehicles that for some reason were descending rapidly.

A text from him: "You're so Kurt-y". Cobain or Vonnegut? (He means Cobain, duh, but I thought I'd entertain the alternative for a moment, pardon me).

Something tells me this is the last leg of our trip. In the football field's parking lot with some lunatic dressed in official high school colors, on a cell, grinning at me like a banshee for some fucking reason. Whatever.

Before I left I got your parcel. Yes, You. I haven't opened it yet. I'm too scared, okay? There. You're special. You're more important than any of these middle class slags. You should know that by now. It's not that I don't want want to talk to you, I just don't know what to say to you right now. You should know that too. (Remember your ultimatum about speaking and love? I do.)

I know what you think of me
so I won't defend or condescend
just know you've got my sympathy

The same geek grins, joined by some fatass soccer mom wearing the same official suburban colors. Kids throw shit on a field. There's not much ice here. Funny (or maybe not) how I loathe those colors the same way I loathe the colors of cops' uniforms. Both incite the same killer instinct.

Are we finished? I hope so. *I* want to be finished.

I feel like pretending to cruise one of these jocks, just for laughs. If he was here and not at work, I would. But then whose laughs would they be?

Meanwhile, on November 1, two of the best currently-creating American artists (I was going to add "queer" to that list of qualifiers, but the word seems even more anachronistic than "artist" does (and, increasingly, "American")) now that the 21st Century is over): Zac Pennington of Parenthetical Girls released the fourth EP in his *Privilege* series, *Sympathy for Spastics*, while Dennis Cooper shoveled out his latest novel, *The Marbled Swarm.*

You might want to consume both.

I'll just keep hanging from the privilege
hanging for the privilege

I do not, nor will I ever, apologize for my privilege.

Haruki Murakami can suck my dick.

This has been a story about an imagined apocalypse that might actually be happening. Thank you for reading.

Brad's Dad

Brad's dad finds Brad's head in the freezer. Goddamnit—he told those motherfuckers not to leave that thing in the house. Brad's dad sighs internally. He's gonna have to get that fucker out of here before—well, no time specifically, but the sooner the better, right? Brad's dad lifts his son's severed head, tosses it between two hands like a frozen ham. He's surprised by how heavy it is. He sets the head down on the kitchen counter—marble, his ex-wife's choice. That sets Brad's dad into fits of reverie and he can't help but sit on the kitchen floor and cry, banging up stray tiles with a hammer.

Brad's dad paces the kitchen, eats a box of Oreos, throws the empty box across the room. He kneels in front of Brad's head, looks into frozen eyes. Weird how Brad seems just as animated dead as he did in life. Brad's dad pushes on Brad's eyeballs lightly with his thumbs. They collapse into Brad's skull with a satisfying ease. Pop. Brad's dad snickers. He was a good boy, all things considered. He's even better now. Brad's dad snickers again, punts Brad's head across the room just like a football. It crashes through the kitchen door onto the patio. Well, at least it's out of the house now. "Let's hope it doesn't dethaw out there." Brad's dad laughs hard. How fucking priceless would that be?

Brad's dad walks into the living room, tears the stereo system from the wall, throws it as hard as he can across the living room. It breaks into a bunch of pieces which Brad's dad stamps over and over until he feels like crying again. Brad's dad grabs a meat cleaver, kicks his way through the broken glass in the kitchen doorframe. Brad's dad goes to work on Brad's skull, bringing the cleaver down, bringing up chunks of Brad onto the hot-as-hell patio. Brad's dad doesn't feel like crying any more; on the contrary. As he rips Brad's skull to bits, Brad's dad feels what many people feel when they drink a beer, or take a huge shit: relief.

Mickey Mouse

I actually considered going to see the bastard in some bizarre twist of logic. *I've never been to a concert before, dude.* I'm standing on the rooftop of my psychiatrist's office and I don't want to go back down there, for my size to be on their scale, so I try to preserve the moment. *Come on, Mikey.* Going to see my dad isn't something I'd ever considered before. Why now? What cocktail of drugs brought me to this place? *Get ready for a new day.* Should I do it?

Mike spits the pen cap across the room and drums on the notebook cover with his fingers. We're out of his mind now. Fuck. Mike stands up, rubs his eyes, glances at the Mickey Mouse-shaped box where he stashes his acid when the phone rings.

"Hey."

"Hey . . . who is this?"

"Is that a serious question?"

Mike's pulling off Mickey's head now and he pulls a sheet of acid out of the hollow body. He tears off two tabs, pops them in his mouth, and tries to zone out on the Brian Wilson poster on his wall but can't.

"hat the fuck—"

"Hey, man. Calm down. I'm down."

"Mikey. Mikey . . ."

The man calling sounds pissed, then he sighs and doesn't sound like anything.

"Do you have a pen? I'll give you the address."

MIke looks around for paper and shit. The speedy tail end of his last acid trip will help with the date until his next acid trip kicks in. He finds his notebook, a pen, flips the notebook open.

"Yeah . . . man. I'm here."

He still doesn't know the man's name and he'd feel weird about asking; fuck it, as long as he's getting paid. He writes down the address the man gave him and puts on a Beach Boys record and zones out on homework scattering the floor across the room and the homework becomes waves and the waves are real and then it's 8:00 and he has to go fuck this guy.

On the way to Queens he remembers how he thought about visiting his father and stares at ads on the train.

The Fog

She doesn't want to say what the metaphor is and I tell her to just tell me it and she says no and I look up from her hand on my bare arm at her eyes which are looking down at her hand on my bare arm. Timothy is watching all this and he is, I think, lounging in a desk chair with his hands folded in his lap, but I can't be entirely sure of his seating position because I'm only seeing him peripherally because I'm looking back at my arm and her hand hovering above it. This is his hotel room.

I tell her again to tell me the metaphor. She says no again but I'm already losing interest because I'm watching Allison's hand holding warm, wet wads of toilet paper and dabbing at cuts on my arm. I can see Timothy peripherally and I can almost feel his eyes on us and that excites me but only in a distant way, the way Allison's refusal to tell me the metaphor is distant, soft and distant, because I'm only seeing and feeling the soft warm toilet paper on my gently bleeding cuts. Staring at her hand wiping blood from my forearm it's really obvious that she's black and I'm white.

I ask Allison what the metaphor is again. She sighs and rolls her eyes.

"It's really stupid," She says. "I shouldn't have brought it up."

"Why . . . not" I ask, watching the watery wad of toilet paper turn red. Allison sighs again.

"Okay, she says. "Okay. Fine. IF . . . and I mean, seriously, IF . . . and this is hypothetical because, Christ, I don't want you to turn into a junkie —

Two years later that's exactly what I did. Later that night we would get drunk, dance, piss in public, and talk about music. "This is where meaning ends," Timothy said at one point, the final line of a poem he improvised. We did that stuff a lot with him, making up poems or reading poems to each other in our school's courtyard, where words I think of when I think of it are leaves and wind and gray. The courtyard is probably one of the only places on the lower east side where *not* speaking in meter would be out of place. I miss it though.

With her hand on my arm Allison finished explaining the metaphor and I nodded. She told me to put some kind of antibiotic cream on my cuts, even though that kind of defeats the purpose of cutting yourself, but then again so does cleaning the wounds. I told her I would do that. I didn't. We were in a Taxi later rolling past stuff and me and Timothy read poetry from a book while Allison listened and I got the feeling she was unhappy and I knew why and I'm pretty sure Timothy paid.

He Turned From the Camera

He was crying. He started walking down the concrete ramp, away from the diner's entrance, crying and smoking. Smoke drifted in front of the lens and his sobs were audible. He sniffed hard, wiped his eyes with the back of his hand, and turned to the camera. His eyes were really red. He took a drag off his cigarette.

"Were you recording that?" He asked quietly.

His droopy, bloodshot, red, tear-stained eyes looked at the DP and he said, "Were you fucking recording that, man?" His voice was shaky.

"Uh, no, man . . ." the DP said quietly. The DP was Frank. He was one of our friends.

"You fucking asshole" he said, sniffing again. You could hear the mucus being pulled up into his sinuses or whatever.

"That was some of my best material."

He turned away from us, and I stared at his back for a second or two and then I told Frank to turn the fucking camera on, now. Frank did. We recorded him as he walked away from us again, lighting another cigarette, his eyes puffy in the lights outside the diner. We had him looking like he was about to cry and with snot dripping down his nose.

That was the end of the shoot for the night.

Scene

His eyes were the first thing we talked about when we heard that Sammy Peterson died. Sammy wasn't hot, really; thin, awkward, and waify, but with a low, guttural voice (you knew it would turn into a smoker's voice one day) and a clumsy manner of speech and movement. Thing is, we all either had or had wanted to fuck Sammy. It was all in his goddamn eyes, which were bluish. Looking into those eyes, we all seemed to agree, sitting around Samantha's bedroom, there was a mixture of emotions none of us were sure how to categorize. Beneath a lightly glazed exterior I saw many things in those pools: deep, immeasurably deep loneliness and sadness and longing and a kind of hurt crying out for anything to ease it.

I had a vaguely notable encounter with Sammy the day before he died. I was at his house to buy a dub of weed, and in the polished wood of his bedroom we got naked like we usually did, and laid beside each other on his bed before he shoved his cock in my mouth, then I shoved mine in his, which he accepted readily, almost deep throating it, moaning, and then he reached under my thigh and stuck what must have been at least been three fingers up my asshole and I came all over his face. Sammy and I laid together again, still but breathing hard. Eventually I got up and put my clothes on and left.

I got high later that night. I must have been high on Sammy's weed at the same time he choked to death. That feels like it should mean something, but it doesn't.

I finally stop staring at the spliff and hand it to Amanda before immediately staring down at the fluffy pink rug we're all sitting on. Justin's call to Samantha about Sammy's death must have only occurred ten minutes ago, tops, but it feels like hours. There's a tightness behind my eyes and my face feels flushed. When I look up at Amanda coughing on Samantha's bed I notice that my eyes are watering a little and my first thought is I wish I could come on those eyes one more time.

Some Might Think

The blister would be the worst part. the blister from a cigarette burn. it's actually the best.

If the cigarette burns your skin straight on, deep and evenly, you'll get a big, watery blister. the color of the blister is a sort of dirty white, almost like what decent dope looks like or you'd imagine a bone to look like. you can see an isolated, grayer part of the blister, which is where the nicotine sticks to its interior surface.

If you wait long enough and then press on the blister, with just one finger, with just a tiny bit of force, it pops.

That pop is the universe. it's everything. pure, blinding white. then it's a leaky crater. and then you go out and do another good one, straight on, another perfect one.

What we said

"**C**heck out this video of this one dude! His friends cut his balls off in his sleep!"

"I can't believe this shit is real."

"I know. It's insane."

". . ."

"Kyle?"

". . ."

"Kyle?"

"Huh?"

"I want to ask you something."

". . ."

"Kyle?"

". . ."

"Ky—"

"Yeah. What is it?"

"What's your favorite part?"

"What?"

"What's your favorite part of the video?"

"I don't know."

"Don't you think this is cool? I mean, like, in a really, really fucked up way?"

"I don't know."

"Here, we'll watch it again."

"No, don't fucking . . ."

"Here. Watch."

". . ."

"So. What's your favorite part?"

". . ."

"Kyle? What's your favorite part?"

". . ."

"Ky—"

"My favorite part is how he's screaming before he's even awake."

"Yeah. See, that's what I thought. That's my favorite part too."

". . ."

"Hehe . . ."

"Man are you seriously watching this again?"

"Haha. Yeah."

"I—"

"Hah-"

"Fuck you. Turn this shit off. Haha. This isn't good enough. Find something more extreme. Show me something more fucked up. Haha. Come on. Get out of here. This isn't fucked up enough. This isn't fucked up enough, you stupid asshole! Okay I'm just joking, haha. Go find something better, haha. Something more fucked up, hahaha. This isn't fucked up enough, haha. This isn't, haha, this isn't fucked up enough. Haha."

The Working Wounded—part 1

We're flying down the road doing who the fuck knows what. I'm too scared to look at the speedometer. The drugs pumping through us, I mean me: an equal mix of acid and ecstasy, with some weed and booze thrown in here and there. I look at Brian, knowing he's probably sober, and this makes me so depressed I want him to crash the car immediately.

The streets drip past us in the manner commonly associated with psychedelic drugs. Lights are painfully bright, zooming past us, and I want to reach over and grab Brian's crotch so hard he slams into a tree or a telephone pole but I take a deep breath, exhale slowly looking at the moon out the windshield.

We're here. Here is a McDonalds in some town I know we've been in but can't recognize. What are we doing driving around in circles? Before I can think of a satisfactory answer to that question Brian is dragging me out of the car by the arm of my sweater. I shake him loose because this is a really nice sweater and I don't want him to stretch it. As he begins to walk away I inhale deeply, but it's too late, he's already in front of me, walking towards the entrance. I sigh and follow him.

In the McDonalds we get in line. I'm not hungry but I can't remember the last time I ate. There's a fat woman in front of me and Brian, and she's dragging her foot over the sticky tiles over and over again. I'm staring at this woman dragging her foot across the floor over and over again when I hear a snap in my ear. I jump, startled, and turn to see Brian staring at me. His blue eyes are pulling toward a place I'm not ready to go and he's not aware he's inviting me to, but that's all quickly washed away when I hear his voice asking, "What do you want?"

Stumbling past Brian, up to the counter, I ask the man at the counter for a number three, large. The man keys some buttons into a computer and tells me the price of the food. Staring directly at a gleaming spot of light on his polished brown forehead I reach for my wallet, take out some bills, and hand them across the counter, never taking my eyes from his head. When the register makes noises and I see, peripherally, that he is extending his arm toward me I look down and take change from his hand. I look at this man's face, his whole face, for the first time, I feel like collapsing, or curling up in a ball and crying. I can't figure out what to do so I stare at the gleaming white counter, dumbfounded. A bag is placed in front of me but I don't have the strength to look at it. A voice from somewhere behind me is saying my name so I grab the brown paper bag and turn rapidly from the counter, not seeing the man as I do so. I begin walking toward Brian. When I reach him, I ask if we're going to eat this here or in the car. Brian's blue eyes tear through my skull as he says, "That's a damn good question."

The Working Wounded—part 2

She walked into the kitchen with a look that would give you a sun tan if she pointed it at you too long. You've never tanned well. You sigh and turn a page in the paper. Sun pours through a window immediately behind you, warming your back and gleaming hard and white off the table in front of you. On the table are your watch and a cup of coffee, and even though you like your coffee black this cup has a hint of skim milk in it because you need to add something cold, just a little bit of something cold, because you don't have the goddamn patience to wait for the cup to cool down on its own and while you're trying to make yourself the master of your surroundings she's sauntered over to the head of the table, across from you, and said, "Can I have a seat?"

Without looking up from your paper you clear your throat and say, "I don't know. Would Brian approve of that?"

She leans the chair's back against her pelvis and you can't not notice the way her hipbones poke through her flesh-colored dress before clinging and twirling and tumbling down her legs into some autumnal design you'll never have a name for. You blink. When she sits down you imagine linguini with alfredo sauce being sucked through her lips.

"What the fuck do you know about what Brian would approve of?"

"Nothing," you say, feeling genuinely apologetic. You don't know the details about Brian's relationship with Sandy and you suddenly feel like you've somehow been set up for a great betrayal, a betrayal of Brian's trust before you and he have even had a chance to start the game, before you've had a chance to do anything. She lowers her gaze and hazel crescents open up to you with the reassurance and warmth of a crocodile pit. Jesus, what am I doing? It's me she's looking at, not you. I can be such an idiot some times.

So, yeah, because this is me and not you, you don't picture what Sandy would look like with shaggy, shoulder-length black hair. You don't wonder what she would look like with a cap on backwards and a bandanna half covering her face. You do want to fuck her cheek bones. I sip coffee and say, "I really don't know much. You know, apart from the job."

"The job? What do you mean "the job"?" she asks while chewing on a metal fork. The hazel crescents roll up at me and register as accusatory, making me stumble over my words: "when I used to know you we were such good friends." "Were we? For a while now, I've been wondering if that's true," she says, taking the fork out of her mouth and stabbing the table with it several times. My face jerks up but I can't look at her face so I look over her shoulder at a porcelain clock with painted bunnies around it on the mantle behind her and things become kind of blurry.

"I mean, we did a lot of drugs. We were basically high all the time." Off screen, I'm sniffling and when we pan over to me I'm playing with my watch (it's my uncle's old Rolex) and wondering what the hell Sandy is babbling about when I realize how exposed we are here, in Sandy's kitchen, how easily her grandmother could call the cops if she wanted to but then I'm just kind of gazing, spacing out, at the little painted animals placed strategically all around the kitchen, and then I hear a buzzing noise in my ear and turn to see to see Brian's face, inches from mine, and I'm looking into his cool blue eyes as he says, "Are we ready?"

"Yeah, of course," I manager to stammer, basically completely petrified due to Brian's presence, and Brian smiles his sexy snake smile and says, "Okay." I put my watch on while Brian walks across past me, to his sister at the other end of the table. I'm putting my watch on and peripherally I see Brian squeezing Sandy's hands and Sandy turns away from him as he kisses her neck and then I'm looking at the time (it's 7:35 (pm)) and trying not to look at Brian or Sandy again. It's hard enough to handle them alone, together it's practically impossible. I look at my shoes.

"When are you guys going to do homework?" Sandy asks. "Are you joking?" Brian responds. Peripherally, I see his feet walking toward me, and then I feel his hand on my shoulder and he says, "Let's go, champ." I stand up, push my chair in, and turn to stare at Brian walking away from me.

Sandy says, "Where are you guys going?"

Brian says, "We need *helicopters*."

Dennis is Scared of His Family

Dennis is scared of his family. He blazed when his father and his brother went out to dinner and felt good, then he felt confused, then he jerked off to thoughts of his retarded uncle. When his dad and his brother got back from dinner Dennis was listening to Eminem on his ipod. He forced himself to speak when his father said something to him and forced himself to eat when food was placed in front of him. After dinner he listened to Eminem some more, ruminated on whether or not he was gay, and opened up his laptop and starting writing about himself and it went kind of like that.

So (on prison)

How do you write about the scariest, most fucked up 48 hours of your life? I was going to start with something like this: "So I set about washing off the filth of that place, the collected grime of bodies stuffed together in cells for days on end, compounded exponentially by the heat and the Heat" before immediately stopping. No, that isn't fucking good enough. Is it really fair that it isn't the '60s any more? No, I don't think it is. "Life's not fair." Seriously, what kind of fucking excuse is that? That's the scariest of all thought-terminating cliches. We can negate that, we have to be able to.

Philip K. Dick wrote an epigraph only he put it at the end of his book. The book was *A Scanner Darkly*. It was a pretty good book. In the epigraph Dick talks about his comrades being punished far too much for what they did, and says that "the enemy" was their mistake in playing. Fair enough, Dick, but what other choice did they have?

Humans lock humans in cages. We seem to take this for granted. Humans with guns and uniforms tell humans without guns and uniforms they'll get a beating at the precinct, and don't you think you won't. What exactly is the punishment for, officer? It's for what you've chosen to do with your body.

To say our bodies are under state control might or might not sound conspiratorial to you but it's hard to deny the validity of that statement. I'd be here all night (I'll be here all night anyway) if I attempted to articulate the absolute dehumanization that is inherent of "the criminal justice system" so I won't. Handcuffed to a wall, I met a junkie who got off with 15 days in prison. He had just done 180 days and was expecting something more along those lines and was ecstatic with the verdict he got. Good for him.

Going to jail forces you to reconsider human beings and where you stand in relation to them. At the end of the day you're a little bit further apart. At the end of the day and the start of a new one, sitting here, writing this, I'm a little bit less human. This is the real punishment, and you can smell it in the air. It's invisible but intense. What was robbed can never be regained, or maybe it can. Who knows? And then you might ask me why I'd want to perma-fried. Kick rocks.

This mind is a burden and all I can do is keep trying to melt it down, down, down.

Hiroshima's Nuts
are in My Vice Clamps

The vice clamps look really nice. they're nailed to the side of my dad's old work bench. the base is painted bright red, and then there are the metal parts—the lever and the clamps themselves. the clamps are black iron or some kind of black metal and the whole set is really, really clean. it looks like the kind of thing a professional murderer would envy, not that i know anything about the feelings of a *professional* murderer. i guess i should talk about hiroshima. between the two clamps his nutsack is purple, rapidly turning blue. hiroshima is indian and he practices parkour. used to practice parkour. those are two of the only things i know about him. oh yeah, and that before he got into parkour he smoked a lot of, and dealt a lot of, weed. oh yeah, and that we used to be friends. and, oh yeah, that this was all before heroin entered my life. it's hard to imagine through hiroshima's wails of pain, but we used to be good friends. we grew up in the same shit new jersey suburb but he went to a different high school than me. then we went to college and then we dropped out of college. this is all really boring and really doesn't matter, so here's the last thing i'll say about the history of me and hiroshima: after we dropped out of our respective colleges and moved back in with our respective parents, we became good friends. end of story. sike. hold your breath like you're dead. or, even better, wail like your nutsack is being crushed. pretend you're looking down your body at the wrinkled, indian brown skin of your sack, and pretend you're watching a vice grip squeezing it. gradually getting tighter. the black metal studs of the clamp permanently destroying whatever tubing links your balls to the rest of your body. now, imagine you're seeing and feeling this. now, react. now, this time, pretend you're a college dropout who got heavy into heroin. pretend you know this kid who used to deal drugs. pretend this scummy, indian, ex-drug dealer, this real piece of shit, pretend he threatens to call the cops. pretend he says he'll do anything to "save" you. he's willing to go to any lengths to stop you from doing heroin. this indian kid, this kid who you don't even know that well, he's going to call the police and tell them where to find your meager stash, your works, everything. now, react. so when hiroshima's nuts explode, it's no surprise that no one's really watching.

A Man Wearing a Three Piece Suit

A man wearing a three piece suit is using a butter knife to saw off the balls of a man who was just wearing khaki shorts and a v-neck t-shirt. a woman should be arriving shortly. the man in the three piece suit has one hand around the other man's balls, pulling them to make the scrotum sack taut, while he uses the other hand to saw at the root of the sack. the other man is, objectively, in extreme pain. subjectively, he's at a place where sea meets mountains. waves rush sand and debris up into this little nook at the base of one mountain where the other man sits. the other man feels the sensation of tugging around his right leg. it's as if an invisible rope is tied to his leg and is being pulled by some unknown force. the man sits up, scattering kelp and seaweed, looks down at his leg, sees nothing, continues feeling the force. he leans back against the barnacle coated wall, confused, hoping the tugging sensation will cease. two hours later it's still going on. the man stands up, paces the nook, sits back down. the tugging is making him frantic, on edge, feeling like he's losing his mind. he just wants it to stop. finally, as the sun sets on the horizon, he picks up a rock and hits himself in the leg with it. he hits his leg over and over again, until the skin tears and blood spurts. the man keeps hitting his leg with the rock until there's a large crater in it. the crater is jagged. shattered gray bone protrudes over the lip of it. the crater looks like it's filled with knots of purple worms, which are actually bruised veins and arteries. raw chunks of bloody skin hang from the edges of the crater like drapes. the man is lying on his side now. he's panting heavily. now he's screaming. his screams get louder and louder. they don't stop.

Some Motel Room in Reno, Nevada

The fleshy taste of turkey, the hard-soft feel of my uncle's cock. For me they've always been inseparable. Probably for my sister too, but I don't know, we've never talked about it. Probably this is just the therapy talking, but probably we should have. Maybe I wouldn't be here, tonight, if we ever did. Then again maybe I would.

The smell of stuffing, the garlicky mush of mashed potatoes. The rotten stench of a stranger's ballsack, pressed halfway to my lips. This was before things became consensual, before he wasn't a stranger any more. I remember being at his house, pressing my hard adolescent cock against his fat arm. This was all after Thanksgiving, though. God, I'm so fucked up.

The smell of stuffing, of gravy, of turkey. The spicy, bleachy smell of his cock. All I can describe turkey as now is: metallic. In some corner of the house, away from everyone eating dinner. "I want to show you something," he said. Nobody paid attention, or maybe they did, I don't know. The point is, I don't know if that's how it tasted to her. Fucked up as it sounds, I wish I knew. I feel like things would have been different if I knew.

The metallic taste of turkey. The metallic taste of his cock. They say that's why I'm gay. Maybe that's why I'm a vegetarian. i'm incredibly high and in some motel room in reno, nevada. but why? why am i here? what made me run away from home on this months long hitchhike across the country (yes, that's why i haven't updated in so long). more importantly, how did i get these drugs and why did i take them? these are answers i don't have questions to.

The only thing keeping me company right now besides this laptop, which i've managed to hold onto, is this ipod, which i've also managed to hold onto. i'm listening to memory tapes. the song is "graphics." Lyrics: "you can be alone even though i'm here by your side." yeah, ipod, tell me about it.

In truth i don't know why i'm listening to this music. i'm almost out of money and i feel like i should be listening to something more, i don't know, edgy, appropriate, tom waits or something. not to call what i'm doing edgy, even though i just did. hey, i guess it kind of is, since i have about fifty bucks left and i probably won't be able to pay for this motel room. time to hit the pawn shop tomorrow.

Being homeless isn't really want i expected it to be. i mean, it's fun at times, but at other times it's confusing, weird, and scary as hell. do i regret it? not really, no, at least not yet, but who knows what the future will bring.

Gotta go panhandle on the street now. i'll update when i have time. if you're reading this mom, dad: fuck you.

A Career Path

"**H**ave you ever considered suicide as a career path?"

Tulip says this to me and I'm not sure what she means, but then I'm thinking, Kevorkian. The doctor will kill you now.

"Well, yeah," I say, "but why should the terminally ill have all the fun?"

Tulip asks, "What?" She says, "No, wait. What I meant to say is, have you ever considered a career path as suicide?"

I stop scrubbing and look up from the soapy water into her face.

"Considered it? I'm living it, baby," I say, and continue scrubbing.

Don Started Smoking

Don started smoking cigarettes the day his cat died. He drove to the local 7-11, asked for a pack of Camel Lights (he remembered his friends in college smoking that brand), and waited until he got back home before he lit one. At home, he seated himself in front of the litter box where his cat, Toby, black, 11, lay dead, and he packed the cigarettes against his palm the way he remembered his friends in college doing, before removing the shrink-wrapped plastic and taking a cigarette out. Toby's head was twisted to the side, his nose and one closed eye buried in the litter, the rest of his body flattened on top of it. Don lit the cigarette with one of the matches he kept above the stove. On the first drag he coughed, but he soon settled into the rhythm of smoking, the steady inhale and exhale, as he let ashes drop by his knees and watched the cat's closed eyes.

The next day Don called his old dealer because he wanted to buy pot. Don hadn't bought pot since he had all his old friends from college and Carol over at his house. Don had never been a big pot fan but he knew his friends were, and he knew Carol would appreciate it. That was two

New Yearses ago and he remembered sitting on the patio with Carol, the two of them passing a joint, and watching the smoke drift through the outside lights and the freezing winter air. He smoked more for her sake than his, and when she turned and smiled at him things happened that he didn't remember any more. Don was lucky his dealer answered after all this time. He told the dealer he didn't know what he wanted, a fifty bag, whatever, and two hours later the dealer was at his house. Don thanked him and closed the door before returning to the litter box. He was almost out of cigarettes by now and he thought about rolling a joint but realized he didn't have any papers. Don didn't feel like going to 7-11 again so he hollowed out an apple and smoked through it, the way his friends in college used to. Don took a few hits before coughing hard and he could feel his eyes watering as he stared at the cat's closed lids.

Don was laying on his back when he realized he'd never done cocaine. All these years, all this time since college, and he'd never once tried it. He called his dealer back but there was no answer. Looking at the time on his phone, Don realized that this was probably because it was four in the morning. This surprised Don, and for a moment he couldn't remember what day it was. The apple near his feet still appeared fresh so he figured it must not have been long since his bought the pot. Looking at Toby's eyes, Don resolved to call the dealer again in the morning, and then he continued staring until he didn't.

Don was awake and it was seven in the morning. Toby's eyes were still closed and he decided to try his dealer again. This time the dealer answered, but when Don asked for cocaine, the dealer said he didn't have any. The dealer instead gave Don the number of someone who could get him the cocaine, and he trusted him with the number because Don was an old friend, and Don thanked him. Don called the number and a half hour later there were three grams of cocaine at his house. Don asked the man with the cocaine if he had any cigarettes, and the man gave him one. Don thanked him. Don brought the cocaine and the cigarette to the floor in front of the litter box. There was a fly on Toby's eyelid and when Don shoed it away he noticed worms crawling in the litter. Don dumped the packet of cocaine onto the floor and, using his credit card, cut it into eight huge lines. A small mound of cocaine was left on the side as Don snorted one line and then another through a rolled up twenty dollar bill. After every line was gone Don stuck the twenty into the remaining pile and sniffed hard. Don felt like he was going to cough, and then he felt like he was going to throw up, but he didn't do either. Don put the cigarette into his mouth and lit it. He was staring at Toby and the worms now writhing against the cat's body, wrapping themselves around his tail. Don could feel his heart beating fast now and he put one hand on his chest, the other hand holding the cigarette between his lips. He opened his phone and wondered how much time was left.

50 Cent: Blood on the Sand (review)

The very first thing the very first loading screen in 50 Cent: Blood on the Sand does is tell you how to turn off the music.

Actually what it says is something about enabling an "orchestral score," which is probably even more hilarious. What kind of depraved dilettante would purchase a game featuring 50 Cent as the protagonist only to turn off the soundtrack, which features an array of hits by 50 himself? In truth the game is only marginally "based" on the legacy, life, and persona of 50 Cent, but that's beside the point. To answer my own question re: who *wouldn't* listen to Fifty's tunes while blasting through hordes of brown people as the titular gangster-turned-rapper: a) white people (specifically white *gamers* who might have heard that, hey, the game is actually pretty good, despite the presence of LOLOMG *50 Cent*), or b) children living with their parents, who, having managed to either sneak the game into the house or convince a half-drunk pill-popping mother to take a break from trying on capris to wander over to the mall's GameStop and slap down some cash and an id for this thing, don't want to risk that same mother overhearing Fitty's rhymes, which are admittedly too real for the average suburban housewife to be exposed to without her screeching about something or other.

Let's get to the point, though: telling us point-blank, before we even have a chance to get to the *opening cutscene*, how *not* to hear the music of the man whose likeness this game is based on is not so much an affront to 50 (either way, he's getting paid) as it is a sad indication of the culture of self-doubt this game was produced and released in. Not even after paying for a 50 Cent-related product can we feel comfortable just sitting with the man's rhymes, maybe nodding our heads a little as we punch an Arab man in the face.

It's the one mark of self-doubt on a game that's otherwise gleefully self-assured and doesn't give a *shit* who knows it. The game begins with 50 concluding the last show of his tour, in an unnamed Middle Eastern City, and dropping his mic for a shotgun literally seconds later, before he even has a chance to leave the venue, for god's sake. He then makes a Middle Eastern man in what must be a backstage dressing room give him a skull encrusted with diamonds; an associate of 50's coolly regards the ice, and 50 seems to appreciate it, as well. Suddenly, though, a bitch steals the skull, and 50 is off on a journey through this bombed-out unnamed Middle Eastern city in an effort to track down the bitch and *get his skull back.*

In an early cutscene, 50's Arab informant informs him on the location of a man he's tracking: "you can find him the club." This is all you need to know about 50 Cent: Blood on the Sand.

Okay, there's also that the game is fucking fun. It's The Club with a plot, Gears of War stripped down (if that's

113

even possible) to its base joys—those being, taking cover and shooting.

What's more, it's an ode to American excesses; a parody of pop cultural irresponsibility; a red-blooded love letter to our absurd world. It is, to paraphrase one forum poster, Gears of War fried in cocaine. In a way, it's an American Killer7.

50 Cent: Blood on the Sand might just end up being the Game of the Year.